NO TURNING BACK

Sneed was dead because of what Slocum had done.

If I had never come to town, this would never have happened, Slocum thought. If I had minded my own business, Sneed would be banged up, but he would still be alive.

Slocum could not remember a time when he had felt so responsible for something like this. It had all happened so quickly. If only— But there was no sense in thinking like that. What was done was done, and that's all there was to it.

Myrtle stood up slowly and turned away.

She knows it was my fault, Slocum thought. She likely hates me for it. She wouldn't be surprised to see me riding down the street on my way out of town. Damn it. Trouble just seems to follow me around. Maybe I should get out before I cause any more harm. He started to walk slowly, but he was following Myrtle.

Slocum knew what he was going to do. He knew that leaving town now was not a real choice . . .

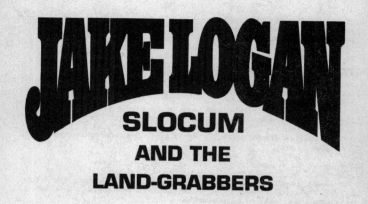

JAKE LOGAN

SLOCUM
AND THE
LAND-GRABBERS

JOVE BOOKS, NEW YORK

THE BERKLEY PUBLISHING GROUP
Published by the Penguin Group
Penguin Group (USA) Inc.
375 Hudson Street, New York, New York 10014, USA
Penguin Group (Canada), 90 Eglinton Avenue East, Suite 700, Toronto, Ontario M4P 2Y3, Canada
(a division of Pearson Penguin Canada Inc.)
Penguin Books Ltd., 80 Strand, London WC2R 0RL, England
Penguin Group Ireland, 25 St. Stephen's Green, Dublin 2, Ireland (a division of Penguin Books Ltd.)
Penguin Group (Australia), 250 Camberwell Road, Camberwell, Victoria 3124, Australia
(a division of Pearson Australia Group Pty. Ltd.)
Penguin Books India Pvt. Ltd., 11 Community Centre, Panchsheel Park, New Delhi—110 017, India
Penguin Group (NZ), Cnr. Airborne and Rosedale Roads, Albany, Auckland 1310, New Zealand
(a division of Pearson New Zealand Ltd.)
Penguin Books (South Africa) (Pty.) Ltd., 24 Sturdee Avenue, Rosebank, Johannesburg 2196,
South Africa

Penguin Books Ltd., Registered Offices: 80 Strand, London WC2R 0RL, England

This is a work of fiction. Names, characters, places, and incidents either are the product of the author's
imagination or are used fictitiously, and any resemblance to actual persons, living or dead, business
establishments, events, or locales is entirely coincidental.

SLOCUM AND THE LAND-GRABBERS

A Jove Book / published by arrangement with the author

PRINTING HISTORY
Jove edition / November 2006

Copyright © 2006 by The Berkley Publishing Group.

ISBN: 0-515-14218-2

JOVE®
Jove Books are published by The Berkley Publishing Group,
a division of Penguin Group (USA) Inc.
375 Hudson Street, New York, New York 10014.
JOVE is a registered trademark of Penguin Group (USA) Inc.
The "J" design is a trademark belonging to Penguin Group (USA) Inc.

PRINTED IN THE UNITED STATES OF AMERICA

10 9 8 7 6 5 4 3 2 1

1

Charley McGuire was in the house when the riders rode up. His wife Ernestine was outside at the well getting some water for the evening meal. The two children were outside playing. They were a boy and a girl, Georgie and Bonnie. They were behind the house watching a green lizard slither up the side of a big oak tree. The riders came up close and stopped their horses quickly, scowling down at Ernestine. She looked up at them with a questioning and worried expression.

"What do you want here?" she asked.

"We want you and your brood out of here," said the man in the lead. He was a man of average height, wearing a black shirt and black hat. He had no whiskers on his face.

"Who are you?" she said.

"Never mind about that," said the man. "Pack up your junk and get out before dark."

"This is our home," Ernestine said. "We filed all the papers. It's legal. You can't run us off just like that."

"We'll pay you. We got the papers all drawn up right here." He reached into his shirt and pulled out a folded paper, which he held out toward Ernestine. "Where's your old man?"

Just then Charley stepped out the front door. He was

holding a shotgun across his chest. "I'm right here," he said. "What's going on here?"

"Like we told your woman," said the leader of the gang, "we want you to pack up and get out of here before dark. I got the papers right here for you to sign. We'll pay you for your property."

"I ain't selling," said Charley. "You can ride on out of here right now."

"We didn't come here to be turned down," said the man in black. "Take this paper and sign it."

Charley had twelve dollars and fifty cents in the house tucked away in an old sock. It was all the money he had in the world. He wondered what the tough man was willing to pay. If it was enough, it might be worth the trouble of a move. Leaving this place with money in their pockets would be better than putting up with this constant harassment. His expression softened a little. "Ernestine, bring me that paper," he said.

"Now you're getting smart," said the man in black as he handed the paper to Ernestine. She took it and glanced at it as she walked over to hand it to Charley. Charley laid the shotgun across his arms in the crook of his elbows as he took the paper to read. His eyes opened wide and he looked up at the man with an astonished expression.

"Twenty-five dollars," he said. "Twenty-five dollars. Is that what you're offering to pay me for this place? Is that all?"

"That's the price," said the man.

"You got to be crazy," said Charley. "Why, the improvements alone is worth more than that. A lot more. And the whole sixty acres—"

"That's the offer," said the man. "Take it and clear out tonight."

"You ain't robbing me," said Charley. He tore the paper in half and tossed it on the ground. He was in the process of shifting the shotgun back into firing position when the man next to the man in black pulled a six-gun and blasted a hole in Charley's chest. He dropped the shotgun and fell back against the door slowly sliding down to a sitting position. His eyes were open, but they did not see. Charley was dead.

Ernestine shrieked and ran toward him, but before she could reach him, the same gunny fired again. His second bullet tore into her back and she fell dead in the dirt several feet away from where Charley sat at the front door.

"Burn the place," said the man in black. Two men dismounted and ran to the house. They went inside. There was a fire in the cookstove, where Ernestine had been getting ready to prepare her meal. One of the men leaned back, raised a leg, and kicked the stove over, spilling out hot coals and burning wood.

"That'll get it," he said. He ran back out the front door. The other man was about to follow, but something caught his eye. He hesitated. He stepped over to the table and picked up a small rag doll. Going back outside, he held the doll up to the man in black.

"Find her," the man said.

Behind the house, Georgie and Bonnie had been watching in silent horror. They heard the order. Georgie grabbed Bonnie by a hand and turned to run. They ran into the thick woods behind the house as fast as their little legs would carry them. The riders moved around behind the house looking for any signs of the girl. They saw none. A couple of them rode a ways into the woods, but they soon came back out. There was a small toolshed behind the house, and one man dismounted and looked inside. There was no one there. Soon the riders gathered again in front of the house, which was by this time in flames.

"Ain't no sign of her," one said.

"She can't be far," said their leader.

"Woods is thick back there," said one.

"She could be at a neighbor's or something," said another.

"There's a shed back there, Amos," said yet another. "Want me to torch it?"

"Yeah," said the man in black, called Amos. "The rest of you keep looking for that kid."

The gang of riders started moving again, around the house, into the woods, some dismounting and poking under brush, searching in vain since the two children were far into the deep woods, still running as fast as they could go. Bonnie was crying. Georgie was crying too, but silently. Tears streamed down his face, but he was being manly. He knew what had happened back at the house, and he knew that he had to take care of his little sister. There was no one else. It was getting hard to catch his breath, and his chest was hurting. He knew that Bonnie was having a hard time, because she was getting harder to drag along behind him. He knew there was a creek up ahead. He had played there before, but his father had told him not to go so far away from the house. He remembered the creek, though. It had a high bank, and down below the bank, there was a small cave beside the water. He thought that would be a safe place for them to hide for at least a while. He kept running, kept dragging his sister, and tried to shut out the sound of her sobs. Once she fell, and he had to stop and help her up and force her to continue.

"I want Mommy," she said.

"They killed her, Bonnie," said Georgie. "They killed Pappa too. I seen it. They're both dead, and if they find us, they'll kill us too. Come on now, Bonnie. We got to get away."

They ran some more until they came out on the far edge of the woods. The creek was just ahead. The high bank was steep, but Georgie knew a way down. He pulled his little sister along until he came to the right spot, and then he sat down on the edge and made Bonnie sit in front of him. He scooted forward until they both started to slide, and they slid on their backsides down to the bottom. The narrow bank down there was rocky. No ground showed through the rocks. They were mostly fist-sized, and walking over them was a little difficult, but Georgie managed to lead Bonnie to the cave. He took her inside, and they both sat down. Georgie pulled Bonnie close to him and held her tight, and then they cried together.

*   *   *

Back at the house, which was by this time almost gone in the flames, Amos sat on his horse holding the doll. The men came riding back to join him. "Ain't seen a sign," said one of them.

"Little kid like that," said Amos, "little girl, she won't last the night. Forget her. Let's go." He rode up close to the flames and tossed the rag doll in to burn. Then he turned his horse and led his gang away.

The temperature dropped in the night, and in the small cave by the creek, the children shivered. They huddled close together now for warmth as well as to console one another. Bonnie at last cried herself to sleep, and Georgie sat holding her tightly and wondering what they were going to do. He was only twelve years old. He wanted to find the men and kill them, but he had no gun. He did not even have his father's guns. They were back at the house. One rifle and one shotgun. He had seen the smoke back behind them while they were running, and he figured the guns were both burned up. He did not think he could kill the men even if he had guns. He had to think about Bonnie. He had to find a safe place for her. He knew that he could not take care of her. He wasn't at all sure that he could take care of himself. He had to think of something. At last he too fell asleep.

Randal Morgan and his wife and family lived closer in to town than did the McGuires. They knew the McGuires, but they did not visit often. There was always work to do around the place, and there was never enough money. Randal managed to feed his family well enough, what with the garden and the hunting, and he raised a few hogs, kept some chickens, and had a few cattle. He had milk from the cows. They managed all right, but it would have been nice to have a little cash now and then.

Randal was in the yard chopping wood for the stove. Tildy was in the house frying eggs and ham for breakfast.

Randal had just split a small log and tossed the halves onto his pile when he saw the children walking toward him. He stopped and stared. They came closer. He recognized them as the McGuire children. What were their names? Georgie. Georgie and Bonnie. That was it. There was something wrong. They shouldn't be out walking this far away from home. He looked toward the house and called out in a loud, strong voice, "Tildy. Tildy, come out here."

Tildy came out with a look of curiosity on her face. She was wiping her hands on a dish towel. She was about to ask Randal what he had called her out for, but she saw the children. They were closer now. She ran to Randal's side.

"It's Charley McGuire's kids," he said.

"Yes," she said. She dropped the towel and ran to meet the children. Dropping to her knees, she put a hand on each of them.

"What's the matter?" she asked.

Georgie tried to answer, but his voice caught. He was trying not to cry.

"Come on," said Tildy. She stood up and got the children one on each side with an arm around each one and started walking toward the house. "Come on in the house. You can tell me all about it later."

Randal dropped his ax and walked to meet them. "What's up?" he said. "What are you two doing out here by yourselves?"

The children were dirty and their clothes were torn. Bonnie started to cry. Georgie sniffled.

"They killed them," he said. "They killed Pappa and Mama."

The Morgans took the McGuire children into the house, where Tildy cleaned them up, gave them clean clothes, and fed them. While she was busy with all that, Randal talked to his own children and told them not to ask any questions. "They're in some kind of bad trouble," he said. "Just be polite. That's all."

As soon as they had finished eating, Randal hitched the

horses to his wagon and drove over to the McGuire place. He found the house burned to the ground. As he drove closer, he saw the bodies. Charley's body was badly burned. Ernestine was lying in the yard farther away from the house. He loaded the bodies into his wagon and drove directly into Charlotte's Town and the sheriff's office. He set the brake on the wagon, got out, and went inside. Mark Townsend was sitting behind his desk. He looked up when Randal stepped inside.

"Hello, Morgan," he said. "What can I do for you?"

"I got Charley and Ernestine McGuire outside in my wagon," said Randal. "They're dead."

Townsend sat up straight. "What happened?" he said.

"They were shot. Ernestine was shot in the back. Their place was burned to the ground. I have their two kids at my house. They walked all the way."

Townsend stood up and walked to the door. Jerking it open, he went outside and down to the wagon to look at the bodies. Randal followed him out.

"Who did this?" Townsend asked.

"I don't know," said Randal. "No one saw it but the kids. Georgie said that someone was trying to make his pa sign some paper. That's all I know that I could say in court, but you know as well as I do who was behind it."

"Now, don't get too hasty," said Townsend. "I'll have to do some investigating."

"And I don't suppose it will lead anywhere, like usual."

"Now, Randal, you got no call to talk to me like that," said Townsend. "You know as well as I do that there ain't a thing I can do without proof. None of the things you and the others have complained about could ever be proved."

"Ain't these two bodies proof enough? They were murdered. Plain and simple. And their house was burned down. You might say a house can burn by accident, and you might say that poor ole Charley was trying to shoot someone when he got it, but what about this helpless woman shot in the back? I call that proof of murder."

"Calm down, Randal," said Townsend. "It's plain

enough that she was murdered. I know that as well as you do. What we don't know is who done it. I'll ride out to your house with you and talk to the kids. We'll see if they can tell us anything about this. What are you going to do about them two bodies there?"

"I'll take them back out to my place and bury them there. I can't afford to pay no undertaker, and I know the kids can't."

"All right," said Townsend. "You ready to go then?"

They went back out to Morgan's place, Randal Morgan driving his wagon and Townsend riding along beside him. They did not talk on the way out. When they arrived at the house, Tildy stepped out to meet them. "Hello, Mark," she said.

"Tildy," said Townsend, touching the brim of his hat. He swung down out of the saddle and hitched his horse to a post in front of the house. Randal drove the wagon a little ways off from the house before climbing down. "I understand you have the two McGuire kids in your house," Townsend said.

"That's right," said Tildy. "They came walking up here this morning, all dirty and tired, their clothes in rags. They'd been out all night, I guess, running and hiding."

"You reckon I could talk to them?"

"I guess," she said.

Just then Randal came walking back up to the house. "I'll bury them out back," he said to Tildy. "I think that ought to be all right. Don't you?"

"I think so," Tildy said. She looked back at Townsend. "You want to come in the house?"

They walked inside and found Bonnie mercifully asleep. Georgie was sitting at a chair against the wall. Across the room, the three Morgan children, a boy about Georgie's age, another Bonnie's age, and a smaller girl, sat quietly staring at Bonnie and Georgie. Randal did not come into the house. Instead, he got his shovel and drove the wagon around behind the house. Inside, Townsend took off his hat. He looked at the children, but he couldn't tell one from another. He glanced at Tildy. She gestured toward Georgie.

"This here's Georgie McGuire," she said. "That's his sister, Bonnie, asleep there. Do you need me to wake her up?"

"Not just yet," said Townsend. He walked over to stand before Georgie. "Georgie," he said, "I'm Mark Townsend. I'm the sheriff."

"I know," said Georgie.

"Do you feel like telling me what happened last night?"

"Some men came to the house," Georgie said. "They shot Mama and Pappa."

"Do you know who they were?"

Georgie shook his head. "I never seen them before," he said.

"If you see them again, will you recognize them?"

"I'll know that one for sure," Georgie said. "I'll never forget him."

"Can you tell me what he looked like?"

"He had a black shirt and a black hat," Georgie said.

"Is that all?"

Georgie nodded his head. Townsend walked to the door. He looked back at Tildy.

"Could be anyone," he said. He walked out and mounted his horse. As he turned to ride back to town, he could hear the sounds of Randal's shovel out behind the house.

2

Slocum rode into Charlotte's Town late that afternoon. It was a town like many others he had seen, yet he had never been there before. It was funny, he thought, how you could ride into a town for the first time and have it look familiar. He rode down the street until he spotted the livery stables. He had gone almost through the town, that establishment being at the far end. There were only a couple of small nondescript buildings beyond it. They could have been someone's homes. They could have been most anything. Slocum stopped at the front of the livery, and a man stepped out to greet him. He was a stocky man, maybe forty years old. His clothes were dirty from work, and he wore a drooping mustache.

"Howdy, stranger," the man said. "Sam Black's the name. This is my place. Something I can do for you?"

"I'd like to put up my horse," Slocum said. "Get him a rubdown and some good feed."

"I'll give him the best care he can get," said Black. "He's a fine-looking animal. Don't suppose you'd want to sell him?"

"Not a chance," said Slocum. He read the prices on a sign tacked to the front of the building and dug in his pock-

11

ets for some money. "I saw a couple of hotels on the way through town," he said. "Which is the best one?"

"I'd say Ballard's. Cost you a little more than the Stopping Place, but it's cleaner. Got better beds."

"I'll stop at Ballard's," said Slocum. "What about a place to eat?"

"Best place is right there in Ballard's."

"That's handy."

"Sure is. Say, how long you going to be staying in town?"

"Can't say right now," said Slocum, "but I'll keep you paid up. Say, who's Charlotte?"

"Charlotte? Oh, she was the wife of the man who started this town. Years ago. The old man's gone, and she is too."

Slocum unsaddled his Appaloosa, took the bedroll, saddlebags, and Winchester rifle, and started walking down the street. The street was crowded. Charlotte's Town was a busy place. He had to cross the street to get to the Ballard Hotel, and in doing so, he had to dodge riders on horseback, wagons, and other pedestrians. He made it safely into the hotel and paid for a room. It was on the second floor. He went up and stashed his gear, then went back down to the eating place. It was crowded, but he managed to find a table. He sat down, took off his hat, and placed it on the empty chair next to him. It was a nice place, even fancy for a town like Charlotte's Town out in the middle of nowhere. In short order, a woman came up to take his order. She was plump, middle-aged, and friendly. He ordered his food and had coffee while he waited, but he didn't have to wait long. He finished the meal and had one more cup of coffee. Then he paid and went outside.

He stood on the sidewalk and looked up and down the street. He could see three saloons from where he stood. One was big and fancy. Another looked like a dump. Slocum chose the one in the middle. It looked like a run-of-the-mill Western saloon, and besides, it was the closest to the hotel. It was across the street, though, and he had to once again dodge all the traffic to get himself over there. He wondered casually as he crossed how many drunks managed to get themselves run over in this town on a Saturday night. When he made it inside the saloon, he was surprised at how few patrons were in there. A couple of cowhands stood at the far end of the bar. Three tables were fully occupied. One was filled with men in business suits. One appeared to be occupied with workingmen. The other one was mixed. It had a couple of cowboys, a man in a suit, and a man in overalls. Slocum walked up to the bar and put a foot on the rail. He dug out some money, which he slapped down on the bar. The bartender came over to meet him.

"What'll it be, mister?" he said.

"A glass of good bourbon," said Slocum.

"Coming right up."

While the bartender poured Slocum's drink, Slocum glanced up at the large mirror behind the bar. He could see everyone in the whole damn place. He saw a man with a badge on his chest come walking into the saloon, and watched as the man moved straight to the table with the mixed crowd. He pulled out a chair and sat down. Slocum picked up his drink and took a sip. It was good whiskey. It had been a time since he'd had any. He took a second sip and set the glass down in front of him. Then he noticed in the mirror that an argument appeared to be developing at the table where the lawman had gone. The man in the overalls was gesturing wildly. Then his voice was raised.

"You can't make me sell out," he said. "Your offer ain't worth dog shit, and even if it was, I ain't intending to sell. It's my place. I got the papers on it. It's my place, and I aim to keep it, so don't be pestering me no more about it."

The man stood up as if to leave, but one of the cowboys, a man in a black shirt and black hat, spoke up to stop him. "I wouldn't be so final about that if I was you," he said.

"What do you mean? You trying to scare me?"

"Now why would Amos want to scare you, Mr. Fog?" said the man in the suit. "Sit down and let's talk this thing over."

"We've done talked it over, and I've give you my answer."

"Your final answer?" said Amos.

"You damn right."

"It might be more final than you mean."

"You hear that, Sheriff? He's threatening me," said Fog.

"I didn't hear no threats," said Townsend. "There's no sense in raising your voice. These men just want to talk business with you. That's all."

"They don't want to talk business," said Fog. "They want me to agree with everything they say. That's what they want. And if I don't agree, they threaten me. A hundred dollars for my spread. I've worked hard on that place. It's worth a hell of a lot more than that. Besides, I don't want to sell it at any price."

"There you go again," said Amos. "Talking without thinking. Now I'm sure that someone could offer you a price you'd take for that tumble-down place of yours."

"Tell you what," said the man in the suit. "I'll double my offer. What do you say?"

"Nosir. I won't take it."

"Triple."

"Triple? I—No. No, it ain't for sale."

"I'll pay five times my original offer, cash, and that's final. What do you say? You're single, aren't you? Got no one to worry about but yourself? You could pack up and be out of there by noon tomorrow. You could be on your way to a new start with five hundred in your jeans."

While he was talking, the man in the suit had pulled out a wad of cash and tossed five one-hundred-dollar bills on the table. Fog was staring at them with wide eyes.

"What do you say, Foggy?" said Amos.

"I ain't never had that much money at once in my whole life," said Fog.

The man in the suit pulled a paper out of his pocket and tossed it on the table. "Just sign this and it's yours," he said.

"You see?" said the sheriff. "No one's threatening you."

Fog sat back down and reached for the paper. "Show me where to sign," he said.

"Right there," said the man in the suit, pointing with a finger. Fog grabbed the pen the man offered and signed his name. Then he reached for the money. He stuffed it into a pocket.

"How soon will you be out?" asked the man in the suit.

"I'll be gone by noon," said Fog. He turned to rush out of the saloon. The man in the suit tucked the paper back into his coat pocket, leaned back, and smiled.

"You ain't paid anyone that much before," said Amos.

"That's all right," the other said. Then he looked at the sheriff. "Mark," he said, keeping his voice low, "who is that stranger at the bar?"

Townsend glanced over. "I've never seen him before," he said.

"He looks like a gunfighter to me."

Townsend looked again. "I'll find out," he said, and he got up and walked toward Slocum.

The man in the suit leaned toward Amos and spoke lower yet. "I've got the property and a witness to prove I bought it fair," he said. "Now I want that money back."

Amos smiled. "I get you," he said. He downed his drink and stood up. "It's getting late," he said. "I think I'll head home and get some sleep. Good night, Mr. Thornton."

"Good night, Amos," said Thornton.

Amos walked out of the saloon followed by other cowboy, who had not said a word the whole time, at least not since Slocum had come into the saloon. Thornton was left sitting at the table alone. He tossed down his drink and poured himself another. Townsend had walked up to stand beside Slocum. He cleared his throat loudly and hooked his thumbs in his belt. Slocum shot him a sideways glance.

"You want something?" he said.

"I'm Mark Townsend, the sheriff."

"All right," said Slocum.

"Who might you be?"

"I might be anyone."

"Don't fool with me, mister," said Townsend. "What's your name?"

"Slocum."

"Just Slocum?"

"Yeah."

"Is that a first name or a last name?"

"It's all the name you're going to get."

"I want to know—"

"Look, Sheriff," said Slocum, "I just stopped off for a rest. That's all. I got a room in the Ballard Hotel across the street. I stabled my horse down at the far end of town. I had supper in the hotel, and now I'm having myself a drink. Is any of that against the law?"

"Well, no, but—"

"Then leave me alone."

"Well, I don't like the way you wear your gun."

"So what?"

"Just remember that I'm keeping my eye on you."

"Which one?" said Slocum.

Townsend sputtered and walked away back to the table where Thornton was sitting.

"I guess you learned half of the man's name," Thornton said.

"He's a smart-ass," said Townsend.

"He might be a good man to have on my payroll," Thornton said. He picked up the bottle and his glass, stood up, and walked over to stand beside Slocum. "Can I buy you a drink?" he said. Slocum looked at him.

"What for?"

"Just being friendly."

"I have a drink," said Slocum.

"What brings you to Charlotte's Town?"

"Just passing through."

"You wouldn't be looking for a job?"

"Nope."

"I pay good wages, bonuses too."

"For doing what?"

"Oh, this and that."

"A little shooting maybe?"

"Maybe. Where you staying?"

"Across the street."

"I could pick up your hotel bill."

"I pay my own way."

"Tell me, mister, uh, Mr. Slocum—"

"Just Slocum."

"All right. Tell me, Slocum, do you have all the money you want, all you'll ever need?"

"I got enough for now."

"There's always tomorrow, next week—"

"Not always."

"You're a hard man to talk business with, Slocum, but if you should change your mind, I can be found most always down the street in my office. Thornton Realty. I'm Thornton. I'll be looking for you."

"Don't hold your breath," said Slocum.

Fog rode toward his house outside of town. It was a little farther out than the McGuire place. He was trying to think if there was anything out there that he should take along with him. He supposed he ought to pack up what few clothes he had, enough to last him till he reached the next town and could buy a whole new wardrobe. He had an old rifle he guessed he ought to take along. With five hundred dollars in his pocket, he had no intention of starting over on another hardscrabble farm. He would abandon all his farm implements. He had no more need of them. There was some food in the house, and he guessed that he would pack up what would keep on the trail. It would take him a few days to get to the railroad. He tried to think of there was anyone he should say good-bye to, but he couldn't think of anyone. He had not gotten that close to any of his neighbors. He was on speaking terms with McGuire and with Morgan, but he felt no need to tell either one of them he was pulling out. Hell, he decided, he would just grab a few clothes, some food, his old rifle, and head on out. He guessed that would tickle old Thornton all right. He'd be well gone way before noon tomorrow. He'd just head on out tonight.

He tried to think of these things, but really all he could think of was the money in his pocket. He'd never had so much money. He tried to think if he'd ever seen so much money. He tried to think of what he would do with it. He would go to the railroad town and buy a new suit of clothes. A real suit. Then he would go to the station and buy a ticket to—somewhere. He wasn't sure just where. San Francisco? Denver? Should he go west? How about Chicago or New York or even St. Louis? There ought to be something in those big cities that a man with five hundred dollars could do, something besides farming. But then, he wouldn't worry about that for a while.

First, he would play around a little. He had earned himself a good vacation. He would hit the big saloons, eat fancy food, and drink expensive booze. He'd have himself some fine women too. Not floozies, but fine, good-looking gals. He would have to be careful, though. He did not want to run through his whole fortune before he realized it. He would play around for a few days, and then he would decide what to do with himself. There was bound to be some kind of business he could set himself up in with that kind of money. He would poke around and see what was needed. Then he would set himself up and start making money. He could see that he had a whole new life ahead of him. Yes, indeed. He was absolutely thrilled. He could hardly wait to get started. He pulled up in front of his house and dismounted. Then he hurried to the door. He flung it open and stepped inside. He had to slow down then, because it had gotten dark. He reached for the lamp on the table, got a match out of his pocket and struck it, and lit the lamp. He put it back on the table and turned, trying to think what to do first, and stopped.

Sitting in a chair in the far corner of the room was Amos. He was smiling, and he was holding his six-gun in his hand. Fog opened his mouth to speak, but Amos's six-gun spoke first. A bullet tore into Fog's chest. He staggered, slumped, and fell forward dead. Amos stood up and walked over to the body. He bent and felt in the pockets until he found the money. He straightened up and stuffed it into his own pocket. Then he moved to the table. He picked up the lamp and tossed it on the floor. The burning kerosene began to spread rapidly. Amos left the house and walked around to one side to get his horse. As he rode away, he stopped once to look back over his shoulder at the house, which was already engulfed in flames.

3

Inside the offices of the *Charlotte's Town Beacon,* Myrtle Gilligan sat behind a desk writing with a rage. Sammy Sneed was cleaning the press, getting ready to set type. Myrtle finished her job and slapped the desk. She shoved back her chair, stood and stretched, and said, "Here it is, Sammy. You about ready over there?"

"I'll be done in a jiffy, Myrtle," he said.

"Good. As soon as you're ready, set this up and run off a copy. I'll be back in by then and look it over."

"Yes, ma'am."

Myrtle walked out of the office and headed for the Ballard Hotel. She needed some coffee and a bite to eat. She had been working all day long, and it was way past time for a break. But Myrtle took her job seriously. She had never known anything but newspaper work, and ever since her father had died a couple of years ago, and she had inherited the newspaper from him, it had been her whole life. And now, there were serious problems in the valley just outside of Charlotte's Town, and it was her town, and because of her newspaper, it was her job to expose the truth about those problems. She would do it too. She had to do it. Sheriff Mark Townsend had already proved that he would not do anything. She knew that Mark was on Jobe Thornton's payroll, and she longed for enough proof to be able to say it in print. All she could say was that he "appeared to be in Thornton's back pocket," or that "Townsend seemed to be siding with Thornton" on this or that issue. Damn, it pissed her off.

Back in the saloon, Slocum decided that he did not care for the company. He downed his drink and called the bartender over. "Give me a full bottle," he said. The barkeep brought the bottle, Slocum paid for it, and started toward the front door.

"Slocum," Thornton called out.

Slocum stopped and looked back over his shoulder.

"I'll be expecting you, Slocum," Thornton said.

Slocum stared at him for another moment, then turned and walked out. He would go up to his room and relax for a while before going to sleep. All he wanted out of this town was a little rest anyhow. He sure didn't need any guff from the likes of Thornton. He was thinking that the man must be some kind of big local rancher, and he must be trying to buy up land. Slocum had overheard some of the talk with the farmer earlier. Thornton had bought that land all right. Everything had been legitimate. But it was just something about the way the man talked, and there was something about the swagger of that other man, the one that obviously worked for Thornton, that Amos, he was called. Slocum had seen a hundred others like him. He tried to put them out of his mind, and he told himself that he would stay the night, get rested up, have a good breakfast, and hit the trail again right after that. There was always another town on down the road.

In the Ballard Hotel's eating room, Myrtle Gilligan had some ham and eggs and three cups of coffee. She was on her third cup, finished with her meal, trying to relax. But her mind was racing. She was thinking about Thornton and his hired gun Amos, about the way in which Thornton was buying up property in the valley. He seemed to want to own the whole area. He was already the biggest landowner anywhere around. Why did he think he needed more? But it wasn't so much that he wanted to buy up land; it was the way he managed to buy it up: intimidating people, frightening people, even killing people. Of course, she couldn't quite say that in her paper. There wasn't any proof that Thornton or Amos or any other Tall T riders had had anything to do with any of the killings that had taken place in the valley over the last several months. It was just that after anyone mysteriously disappeared, died, or was murdered, Thornton somehow managed to wind up owning their land.

And then there was that Mark Townsend, who kept pestering her to marry him. She couldn't stand Mark Townsend. He was paid to be the sheriff, but he had not come up with anything, not a shred of evidence, for any of the wrongdoings that had taken place in the valley. He threw a drunk in jail now and then. He'd even helped a little boy find his lost dog one day. He had a big smile, and he wasn't bad-looking either. But he made Myrtle sick to her stomach, the way he backed up Jobe Thornton, the way he sided him every time the man came to town, the way he sat and drank whiskey with him, laughing at all his jokes, smiling and bobbing his head. And then he dared to come around again and ask her to marry him.

She finished her third cup of coffee, paid, and walked back to the *Beacon* offices. Sammy had just finished running off the page, and he lifted it off the press and held it up for her to see. "That's good, Sammy," she said. "Lay it over here on the table." Sammy did as she told him, and stepped back to admire his handiwork. Myrtle read over it with a wrinkle on her brow.

Remember the old Know Nothing Political Party of a few years back? Well, I think we have a new political party right here in our town. It's called the Do Nothing Party, and its champion is our own Sheriff Mark Townsend.

Six months ago a hardworking, prosperous farmer

by the name of Cyrus Blanding was working in the valley. He vanished. He told no one he was leaving. He just disappeared. Then one morning, Jobe Thornton showed up with the papers to Blanding's farm. Is that suspicious? Our Do Nothing Sheriff never found anything suspicious about it. He says that he investigated but that Blanding just "up and left these parts."

Tom Jordan was killed at his place about six weeks later. Again, Thornton showed up with the papers. Again our Do Nothing sheriff found no evidence of any kind. "Some passing stranger must a done the dirty deed," he said. "Likely he's in Mexico by now."

That's not the end of it, my friends. Now Charley and Ernestine McGuire, the parents of two small children, have been murdered at their own home, a dastardly deed if ever there was one, to take the parents away from two small children, to leave two small children orphaned. And for what? To get their land? Is that the reason? Will Jobe Thornton show up in town with papers on that place as well? And will Do Nothing Mark Townsend continue to do nothing? How long are we, the citizens of Charlotte's Town, going to allow this to go on?

But what, you may ask—what can we do? I'll tell you. We can start by electing a real lawman for sheriff, someone who will really investigate, someone who will get to the bottom of all the wrongdoing and the evil that is engulfing our lives. We can run Mark Townsend out of town on a rail. That would be a good starting place.

"Don't you think that maybe it's a wee bit strong, Myrtle?" said Sammy Sneed. "It kind of points fingers, don't it?"

"Kinda," said Myrtle.

"We still got time to print up a new page."

"Print this one, Sammy," Myrtle said. "Just like it is."

• • •

Slocum sat alone in his hotel room sipping the good brown whiskey. There was nothing wrong really. It was just that he didn't like being run out of a saloon. Of course, he wasn't really run out. He chose to leave because of the company. He didn't like the people that he found in there. And it didn't really matter. He had already decided that he wouldn't hang around this place for long. That was the one thing about his life that he liked. If he hit a town and found it to be distasteful, he could just keep going, move on to the next one. He could take a job and stick around or not. It didn't matter one bit. Slocum was as free as a man could get. He liked it that way. He had come out of the Civil War some years ago not liking people very much, so when he met new people he was never disappointed. Now and then he was pleasantly surprised. Now and then he ran into nice folks. Now and then. He heard voices outside and the sound of horses starting to move. He got up and walked to his window to look out on the street, and he saw Thornton and a couple of cowhands mounted up and starting to ride out of town. Good riddance, he thought, and he went back to the bed to try again to relax.

Slocum had thought that he would sleep late in the morning, since he had a comfortable bed, and he would get up and have a leisurely breakfast and then leave town. That's what he thought. But street noises woke him up. He moaned, stretched, and got out of bed, walking to the window to look out. There were already people walking up and down the street, men on horseback riding, a few wagons rumbling along, but the thing that had really called him out of his deep sleep was a man on the street calling out for people to buy newspapers. Slocum stood there watching for a moment. People were buying the papers. Well, he was awake. He decided to go on down to breakfast and get on out of town. In another few minutes he was dressed. He had his bedroll and his Winchester tucked under his arm and had walked down the stairs. He stopped by the front door and looked out. There was the man with his bundle of papers, waving one in the air and calling for people to buy. Slocum was about to turn and walk into the eating room when he recognized the man called Amos from the night before. Amos, wearing a black shirt and a black hat, rode up right in front of the man selling papers. He stopped his horse. Slocum stepped out onto the board sidewalk to watch.

Amos dismounted and walked over to stand in front of the man. He tossed a few coins on the sidewalk. "I'm buying them papers," he said. "All of them."

"That's not enough money to buy them all," the man said. "Besides, they're for distribution, not to be bought all up like that."

Amos slugged the man, knocking him over backward and scattering the papers. Then he started gathering them all up. The man curled up on the sidewalk holding his face. Slocum dropped his roll and started walking. Amos was busy gathering newspapers and did not notice that Slocum was right behind him. He picked up the last paper and turned, startled to see Slocum standing there so close.

"Help the man up and give him back his papers, Amos," said Slocum.

"What—"

"Amos is your name, ain't it?" said Slocum. "I heard you called that last night in the saloon."

"Yeah. It's Amos."

"Well, then, help the man up and give him his papers."

"I bought these papers."

"That ain't the way I heard it."

"Mind your own business if you know what's good for you. Now get out of my way."

Slocum swung the butt of his Winchester and smacked Amos across the side of his head. Amos dropped like a rock. The papers dropped again, blowing in the breeze. Amos held the side of his head and moaned. Slocum cranked a shell into the chamber of the Winchester and pointed its muzzle toward Amos.

"Get up, Amos," he said.

Amos turned and looked at the Winchester. He was no fool. He forced himself up to his feet. Pulling his hand away from the side of his head, he looked at it and saw blood on it.

"You son of a bitch," he said.

"I've been called that before," said Slocum. "Now wipe off your hand and pick up the papers."

Amos wiped the blood off his hand on the leg of his trousers and started to pick up the papers. The man who had been selling the papers stood up now and watched wide-eyed. Amos had all the papers in his hands again, and Slocum nodded toward the other man.

"Give them back to him," he said.

Amos handed the stack to the man.

"I think he paid for one copy," Slocum said.

The man handed Amos a copy.

"All right," said Slocum. "You can go now."

"You'll be hearing from me, mister," said Amos, reaching for his saddle horn.

"I don't think I give a shit," said Slocum.

Amos turned his horse and lashed at it, racing away out of town. Slocum turned to walk back to the hotel. He still hadn't had his breakfast.

"Wait a minute, mister," said the man with the newspapers.

Slocum turned back toward the man.

"I want to thank you for what you done," the man said. "I'm Sammy Sneed. I work for the *Beacon*. That's the *Charlotte's Town Beacon*."

He held out his hand and Slocum shook it. "Slocum," he said. "I just don't like bullies. That's all. Excuse me."

He turned and walked back to the hotel and went inside, retrieving his blanket roll as he went. Inside the hotel, he found a table in the eating room where he could sit and watch the door, and sat down. In a moment, a waiter appeared. Slocum ordered coffee, bacon, potatoes, eggs, biscuits, and gravy. The waiter left and in another moment returned with the coffee. Slocum sat quietly, sipping coffee and waiting for his breakfast. The coffee was good. In another few minutes, the waiter returned with the breakfast. Slocum tore into it. For days he had been eating his own cooking on the trail. He hadn't had anything this good in a while, and he enjoyed it. When he had finished, he had more coffee. Even the coffee was better than what he fixed for himself at a campfire. He was about to get up and pay for his meal when he saw Sammy Sneed coming into the room accompanied by a good-looking young woman. They headed straight for his table.

"That's him," he heard Sammy say.

They came on over to the table where Slocum was sitting, and the lady held out her hand. Slocum stood and took it and held it. It was a nice hand, and it was attached to a nice body. In fact, she was a good-looking woman all over.

"Mr. Slocum," said Sammy, "this is Miss Myrtle Gilligan."

"How do you do, Miss Gilligan," Slocum said.

"Please call me Myrtle," she said.

"All right, Myrtle," said Slocum. Then, suddenly embarrassed, he released her hand and gestured toward a chair. "Won't you sit down?"

Myrtle and Sammy each sat, and then Slocum resumed his seat. "I wanted to meet you," she said. "Sammy told me what you did. Thank you. May I buy your breakfast?"

"Oh, no, ma'am," said Slocum. "I'm all finished here. I was just about to pay up anyhow. And I—well, I never let a lady pay."

"I'm no lady, Mr. Slocum. I'm a businesswoman. I own the *Charlotte's Town Beacon*."

"She's my boss," said Sammy.

"Well," said Slocum, "in that case, okay, and thank you."

"Mr. Slocum—"

"Excuse me," he said, "but since we're being so honest and all here, just Slocum will do fine, uh, Myrtle."

"All right," she said. "Slocum. Do you always go to the rescue of the underdog?"

"I guess I really ought to learn to mind my own business," he said. "I'm leaving town here in a few minutes. That is, that's what I had planned on doing. But I just can't stand a bully. Never could."

"Well, I'm certainly glad of that," she said.

"Me too," said Sammy.

Myrtle turned to Sammy. "Don't you think you ought to get back to selling the papers?" she said.

"Oh. Oh, yes, ma'am," he said. "I'll get right on it."

He got up to leave, but she stopped him. "Leave one paper," she said.

"Yes, ma'am," he said, and he slipped one off the top of the stack and put it down on the table. Then he turned and hurried out of the room. Myrtle looked at Slocum and smiled.

"I just thought you might like to have a look at this and see what made Amos so mad," she said.

4

"That's pretty hot stuff," Slocum said. "I'm not surprised that ole boy tried to grab up all your papers."

"Do you know who he was?" Myrtle asked.

"I don't know a soul in this town," said Slocum.

"Well, everyone in town knows you now," she said.

"It don't matter. I'll be moving on."

"Where you headed?"

"No place in particular," said Slocum. "I'm just a drifter. That's all."

"In that case," said Myrtle, "I'd suggest that you drift on out of here pretty damn quick. That man you humiliated out on the main street of town was Amos Dean. He's Jobe Thornton's right-hand man. He'll be out to kill you before you can saddle your horse."

"Others have tried it before," said Slocum. "If that's what he wants, he's welcome to give it a go."

"How would you like to hang around this town, Slocum?"

"I don't think so. I ain't looking for trouble."

"You sure bought into a passel of it just a while ago."

"I wasn't looking for it. I just don't like bullies. That's all."

"This town is being bullied to death," she said.

"It ain't my problem."

She stood up to leave. "I guess I can't blame you," she said. "Thanks again for what you did for Sammy. Good riding."

Slocum stepped out onto the street and looked up and down. He saw Sammy Sneed down toward the livery stable hawking his papers. He seemed to be doing pretty well. Several men bought a copy each while Slocum was looking. He decided to go up to his room and pack and get on out of this town before the trouble caught up with him, as it was bound to do if he stayed around much longer. He turned and walked back into Ballard's, and then he heard a shot, a rifle shot, it sounded like. His curiosity got the better of him and he went back out the door. Down where Sammy had been selling papers, he saw a small crowd gathered. He heard voices raised. He did not see Sammy. Someone was running fast toward the sheriff's office. In another minute, Sheriff Mark Townsend came strolling out of the office and started toward the crowd. He did not seem to be in a terrible hurry. Slocum waited and watched.

Townsend made it to the crowd. It looked, from a distance, like everyone was trying to talk to Townsend at once. He was waving his arms around trying to quiet them down. Then Slocum saw Myrtle Gilligan come out of the newspaper office and run down the street toward the crowd. Slocum's curiosity really got the best of him then. He started walking that direction himself. As he got closer, he could make out what people were saying.

"Did anyone see the shooter?" Townsend said.

"Well, no, I never seen him."

"I think he was over thataway."

"Did you see him?"

"No, but hadn't you oughta go look?"

"He's long gone by now," said Townsend.

"You know who it was," said Myrtle. Her voice rang out clear. There was no mistaking it. "You don't mean to catch him."

"Now, Myrtle," said Townsend. "You're just upset. You

don't mean what you're saying. Why don't you just gather up your papers and go on back to your office. I'll take care of things here."

"You'll take care of them all right," she said. Then she disappeared from Slocum's view. He was close by this time, and Myrtle had knelt down. Slocum pushed his way through the crowd to see Myrtle kneeling beside the dead body of Sammy Sneed. Newspapers were strewn around. Slocum felt a sudden flood of guilt rush over him. Sneed was dead because of what Slocum had done. He knew that. And he knew that Amos had done the deed. If I had never come to town, this would never have happened, Slocum thought, If I had minded my own business, Sneed would be banged up, but he would still be alive. The crowd began to drift apart. Townsend sent someone to fetch the undertaker.

Slocum stood there watching, feeling wretched. He could not remember a time when he had felt so responsible for something like this. It had all happened so quickly. If only—But there was no sense in thinking like that. What was done was done, and that's all there was to it. A gaunt man in a black suit appeared on the scene, and Myrtle stood up slowly and turned away. She found herself looking into the face of John Slocum. She walked around him and headed toward her office without speaking.

She knows it was my fault, Slocum thought. She likely hates me for it. She wouldn't be surprised to see me riding down the street on my way out of town. Damn it. Trouble just seems to follow me around. Maybe I should get out before I cause any more harm. Maybe—

He started to walk slowly, but he was following Myrtle. He knew what he was going to do. He had no other choice. Leaving town now was not a real choice. He knew that he could not do it. His brain raced with thoughts as he walked the path to the newspaper office. When he reached the door, he stood outside for a moment. Then he took a deep breath and opened the door. Stepping inside, he saw Myrtle at her desk, her head down and in her hands. Her elbows were on the desk. She looked up when she heard the door, and Slocum saw that her eyes were red and tears were running down her cheeks. When she saw him, she wiped her face with her sleeves and sat up straight.

"I thought you'd be on your way out of town," she said.

"No," said Slocum. "I just thought—"

"That you'd stop by to tell me how sorry you are?"

"No, ma'am," he said. "Of course, I am sorry that it happened. But that ain't why I stopped by."

"What then?" she said.

"I come by to ask you for a job," Slocum said. Myrtle's jaw dropped, and Slocum went on. "You don't have to pay me much," he said. "In fact, you don't have to pay me at all. Just tell folks that I'm working for you. I just want an excuse to hang around for a while. That's all."

"Do you know what you're letting yourself in for?" she said.

"I sure do now," he said. "That shooting just now would never have happened if it hadn't been for what I done. I can't run out now. If you don't want to take me on, I'll just hang around on my own."

"No," she said. "No, I mean, I'll hire you. I can't pay much, but I can pay you what I was paying—Sammy."

"I don't need that money. Put it in a bank account, or hide it in a coffee can. Whatever you do with your money. All I want is to be able to say that I'm working for you."

"All right," she said, "but I can save you some money. I have a room in back that you stay in. It's not much but—"

"It'll do just fine," he said.

Slocum went back to the hotel and paid his bill. He packed up his few things and carried them back to the newspaper office, and there, Myrtle showed him the back room. Like she had said, it wasn't much, but it would do. It had a bed and a table, a chair and a nightstand with a water bowl and pitcher. What more did he need? All he would do there would be to sleep some nights. He tossed his roll on the bed and propped his Winchester against the wall in a corner of the room.

"What now?" asked Myrtle.

"I'd like to read that paper again," Slocum said.

She got him a copy and he sat down to go over the story again. He read it twice. Then he shoved it aside. He looked up at Myrtle.

"So three people have been killed," he said, "probably four, and this Thornton has come up with the property of two of them."

"Don't forget Sammy," she said. "He makes five."

"I ain't forgetting Sammy," Slocum said. "I was just counting them that had property."

"That's right," she said. "Three dead for sure. Cyrus Blanding just disappeared, but Thornton got his place, and so I figure he's been killed like the others."

"Seems like I was in the saloon yesterday and this Fog sold his place to Thornton. He got a good price. Thornton paid him in cash."

"But he was killed last night," said Myrtle, "and the cash was never found."

"Anyone could have done it just to get the cash," Slocum said. "It was no secret he had all that money on him."

"You sound like Mark Townsend," she said.

"No, I'm just thinking in terms of evidence. Of course Thornton had it done, and likely he had that Amos do it for him. With everything else that's happened around here, it's all pretty obvious. But you can't take 'pretty obvious' to court."

"Oh, I know that, but—"

"You know what I'd like?" said Slocum, interrupting her.

"What?"

"I'd like it if you would slow down on your editorials for a spell."

"I have to write the truth," she said, "as I see it."

"You don't have to write it every day," Slocum said. "Just ease off for a bit. Please."

"Why?"

"Maybe they'll back off a bit. Maybe they'll leave you alone. If so, it'll give me time to nose around a bit. You've got things pretty hot for Thornton just now. Let him stew for a spell. If he thinks you're laying off, maybe he'll lay off for a while."

"Oh," she said, exasperated, "I'm just itching to write something about what happened to Sammy. It's the closest I can come to taking a gun out to shoot someone."

"Write Sammy a nice obituary. Say he was gunned down in the street by an unknown assailant. Ain't that the way they write them? Don't make any accusations or anything like that. Go ahead and write up what it is you want to write, but tuck it away somewhere and sit on it for a time. It might not be too long. We'll see."

"All right," she said.

"Right now I'd like to see everything you've got on Thornton and that damned Amos Dean, and anyone else connected with them. And how about your sheriff? You got any background information on him?"

Myrtle began to realize just how serious Slocum was about this business, and she began to see that he was working methodically at it. She decided that maybe he was right in his approach. Dig deep. See what you can find out. When you've got the goods on them, then hit them right square between the eyes with it. All right, she decided. She would hold off with her hot editorials. She would be patient, give Slocum some time, and she would help him all that she could. Together they would get that no-good Jobe Thornton and his gang of killers. They'd wipe them all out or put them away for good. She started digging into her files and through old stacks of the *Beacon* for stuff for Slocum to read.

"You goddamn fool," Thornton was saying to Amos Dean, "don't you think it's pretty damned obvious to anyone just who it was went and killed Sammy Sneed? You'd just had a run-in with him and that Slocum. Then right after that, someone drops Sneed with a rifle shot. Who the hell else is anyone going to suspect? You're the only one. You. Just you. Goddamn it."

"They might suspect me, but they can't prove nothing. No one saw me. I made sure of that. Besides, who the hell's going to investigate? Townsend?"

Amos guffawed, but Thornton shut him up.

"It ain't funny," he shouted. "Townsend can only go along with us so far. When people get fed up with what we're doing and enough of them has decided that it has got to be us that's been doing it, they'll all get together and come after us. We got to lay off for a while."

"Not till I get that son of a bitch Slocum," said Amos.

Thornton jumped up out of his chair and pointed a fat finger at Amos just a couple of inches away from Amos's nose. "You don't do anything," he said. "Not till I say so. Don't go off half-cocked on your own again. When I say kill, then you kill. When I say burn down a house, you burn it down. But you don't do anything without my say-so. Have you got that?"

"You don't own me, Thornton," said Amos. "I've never let a man talk to me like that and get away with it. I've killed men for a lot less."

"And no one's ever paid you half as well as I'm paying you. Is that right?"

Thornton waited a moment, but Amos did not respond.

"All right then. If you like my money, you'll do things my way. All right?"

"All right," Amos said. "I won't kill Slocum. Not just yet."

"Not just yet," Thornton repeated. "But don't worry. The time will come, and the more time we let go by, the less he'll be looking for it. Right?"

A slow grin spread across Amos's face. "Yeah," he said. "That's right."

Slocum was still buried in his studies, and Myrtle was at her desk writing, when Mark Townsend walked in. Myrtle looked up and frowned. "What do you want here, Mark?" she said coldly.

"I just stopped in to tell you how sorry I am about Sammy," Townsend said.

"He never hurt anyone in his whole life," said Myrtle. "He didn't deserve that."

"I know," said Townsend, shaking his head and holding his hat in his hands. "It was a terrible thing."

"You know who did it, Mark," Myrtle said. "Why don't you do something about it?"

"Myrtle, I don't know. No one saw the shooter. You heard me ask them all. No one saw it. I can't just go running off after someone on suspicion."

Slocum looked up from his reading. "I heard someone say that the shot came from right across the street," he said. "He even pointed. I never saw you go over there to take a look around."

"The shooter was long gone by that time, and just what are you doing here anyway?"

"He's working for me," said Myrtle.

"What?"

"You heard me, or do you need to wash your ears out?"

"Doing what?"

"I don't think that's any of your business, Sheriff," said Slocum.

Townsend turned from Myrtle and strode over to just across the table from where Slocum was sitting. "You got any newspaper experience?"

"I don't think that's any of your business either. The lady's done give me the job."

Townsend turned back toward Myrtle again. "I don't like this," he said. "There's something funny going on here, and I don't like it."

"Mark," said Myrtle, "you don't have to like it. You don't own this town, and neither does Jobe Thornton. I run my business the way I want to run it. I hire who I want to hire. As long as I don't break the law, it doesn't concern you. So take your phony sympathy and get the hell out of here."

"Well, you'd just better think about what you're doing," Townsend said, and he turned and went out of the building.

"I'd like to smash him like a bug," said Myrtle.

"Take it easy," said Slocum. "You came close to saying too much."

"You told me not to write. You didn't say anything about talking."

"I think it would be better if you kind of eased off there too," Slocum said.

Myrtle stomped across the room and back again. Then she whirled to face Slocum and held up her hands in a gesture of surrender.

"Okay," she said, "you win. I'll keep my mouth shut. You're the boss."

"No," said Slocum, "you're the boss. I'm just making suggestions."

5

Slocum went to the land office and asked to see the records of all land transfers for the last few months. The clerk eyed him suspiciously.

"And just who are you?" he asked.

"Ain't they public records?" asked Slocum.

"Well, I reckon they are, but still we like to know who it is that's snooping around here."

"I could be looking to buy me some land," said Slocum.

"Well, are you?"

"I said I could be."

"What's your name?"

"Name's Slocum. How about those books?"

"Well, now, Slocum, you ain't from around here, are you?"

"What's that got to do with it?"

"Whenever we say that something around here is a public record, we mean for our public. You know what I mean? What I mean is that we don't open up our books for just any drifter who comes riding through town. We'll show them to any local citizen who asks for them, but not to just any stranger."

"I might be a stranger to you," Slocum said, "but it happens that I'm employed by the *Charlotte's Town Beacon,* and I'm claiming the privilege of the press. That's in addition to claiming that public records means just what it says. They're open to the public. Now are you going to bring out those record books, or do I have to get tough with you?"

The clerk looked at Slocum real good and decided that he did not want to tangle with the man. He grumbled something under his breath and turned and walked back to the shelves behind him. In another minute, he came back to the counter and laid out two large books. "Here's what you want," he said.

"Thank you," said Slocum, opening up the first of the two books. He had turned a few pages before he came to an entry that stopped him. He took out a small pad from his pocket and a pencil and made a note. He kept looking. The clerk ambled back into the shelves and then slipped out the back door. Once outside, he ran like hell to the office of Sheriff Townsend. Townsend looked up in surprise as the clerk burst through his front door.

"Elgin," he said. "What's wrong with you?"

"Slocum," Elgin said. "He said his name was Slocum."

"I know him," said Townsend. "What about him?"

"Said he was working for the *Beacon*."

"Well, unfortunately, that's true enough. I just found out a little while ago."

"Well, he come into the land office demanding to look at the records. All the land transfers of the last three months, he said. I tried to hold him off, but he threatened me."

Townsend stood up slowly. "Oh, yeah?" he said. "He threatened you, did he? Where is he now?"

"Still looking at the books, I guess. I sneaked out the back door."

"Let's you and me take a stroll down to your office," Townsend said.

He walked to the peg on the wall where his hat was hanging and took down his hat and put it on his head. Then he hefted his Colt. He drew himself up and sniffed a deep breath. Then he walked to the door and opened it, stepping outside. Elgin was right behind him, and he closed the door. Then the two men walked side by side back down to the land office. Elgin opened the door and stepped aside. Townsend stepped in, Elgin following close. This time, Elgin did not bother closing the door. Slocum glanced up from his studies. He looked back down and finished making another note in his notepad.

"Slocum," said Townsend.

Slocum did not bother looking up again. "I'm right here," he said.

"I want to talk to you," said Townsend.

"So talk."

"I'd like to have your attention."

Slocum heaved a heavy sigh and slapped his pencil down on the counter. Then he turned to face Townsend, looking the sheriff right in the eyes. "All right, Sheriff," he said, "I'm listening. Have your say. Are you going to tell me that it's against the law for me to be in here reading through these records?"

"You know they're public information," said Townsend. "That ain't what I'm here to talk about. Elgin here says that you threatened him. What do you have to say about that?"

"Well, I guess that was the only way I could get him to let me look into these here public records," Slocum said.

"If you felt like he was denying you access to something you had a right to see, you should have come to see me. Not threatened him."

"I ain't seen you do much about anything," said Slocum.

"Come on," Townsend said, jerking his head toward the door.

"Where we going?" Slocum asked.

"We're going to jail."

"For what?"

"For threatening this man."

"You going to put me in jail for saying—" Slocum hesitated. He looked at Elgin. "What was it I said?"

Elgin drew himself up. "You said, 'Am I going to have to get tough with you?' That's what you said."

Slocum looked back at Townsend. "Is that a threat?" he asked.

"Sounds like it to me," said Townsend. "Let's go. Oh, maybe you'd better hand over your Colt."

"I'll go to the jail with you," said Slocum, "and I'll hand you my Colt when we get there."

"Well, all right. Come on then."

They walked to the sheriff's office, Elgin standing on the sidewalk and staring after them. Once inside, Slocum pulled out his Colt and flipped it around to hand it to the sheriff butt-first. Townsend took it and put it in a desk drawer. Then he took up the ring of keys from off the top of his desk and headed for one of the two cells inside the office.

"You really going to go through with this?" Slocum asked.

"It's against the law to threaten someone with violence," said Townsend. He swung open the door and made a gesture for Slocum to step inside. Slocum walked into the cell, and Townsend shut the door and locked it after him. He walked back to his desk and sat down behind it.

"How long do you think you can hold me for that major offense?" said Slocum.

"I'd say at least till the judge shows up."

"When you expecting him?"

"Don't know. He usually comes around every month or so. He was here a week ago."

"Will you go tell my boss that you've got me in here?"

"I ain't obligated to do that."

"Just what are you obligated to do?"

"I do my job," said Townsend. "Uphold the law."

"So you throw me in jail for asking a simple question, and you let that Amos fella walk off after he went and punched poor Sammy Sneed right out there on the main street in broad daylight."

"I didn't see the punch," said Townsend, "and no one made a complaint."

Just then Myrtle Gilligan burst through the front door. "What the hell is this all about?" she demanded.

"That ain't no way for a lady to be talking," said Townsend.

"Just answer my goddamned question," said Myrtle.

"I'm glad you come by," said Slocum. "The sheriff here just told me that he didn't have to go tell you that he had me locked up in here."

Myrtle stomped over to the cell and looked in at Slocum. "Maybe he don't have to, but it would have been common courtesy," she said. She whirled around again to face Townsend. "Now what the hell is going on?"

"I've arrested Slocum," said Townsend.

"What for?"

"For threatening Elgin," said Townsend. "That's what for."

"For threatening—"

"That's what I said."

"How long you going to hold him?"

"Till the judge comes to town and we can have a trial."

"For a threat? You can't do that."

"I can, and I have."

She walked back to the cell and looked at Slocum again. "Did you threaten Elgin?" she asked.

"I guess I did," said Slocum. "They both said so."

"What did you threaten to do to him?"

"Well, now," said Slocum, scratching his head in puzzlement, "I don't think I actually said just what."

"What did you say?"

"I think I said, 'Am I going to have to get tough with you?' Something like that."

"That's it?"

"Near as I can recall."

"That's it," she said, and she paced the floor.

"It's against the law to go around making threats," said Townsend.

Myrtle suddenly spun around and pointed a finger right

at Townsend's nose. He stepped back a bit startled. "Exactly what did Slocum say to Elgin?" she asked.

"Well, pretty much what he just told you."

"You were there?"

"No, but Elgin came to get me, and he told me what Slocum said."

"All right. What was it?"

"He said 'Am I going to have to get tough with you?' That's what Elgin told me he said."

"I got you, you ignorant son of a bitch. Slocum never made a threat. He just asked a question. That's all. Now, if he had said, 'I'm fixing to get tough with you,' then that would have been a threat. If you'd ever have finished school, you'd know that, and I'll bet you my business that the judge knows that. And when the judge throws your whole case right out of court, I'm going to turn around and sue you for false arrest, for damage to my business, and for anything else I can think of between now and whenever the judge shows up. Get ready to lose your job and your pants, Mark."

"Wait a minute, Myrtle," said Townsend, suddenly very nervous, "let's talk this out."

"I've done my talking," she said.

"Is that right what you said?"

"I said quite a bit, and all of it was right."

"I mean about the threat, or whatever it was that Slocum said."

"It was not a threat. It was a simple question. It's a matter of English grammar."

"Damn it," said Townsend. "I never did do any good with English grammar. Elgin said that he'd been threatened. That's all I knew about it."

"You could have opened up a law book and read it," said Myrtle. "That is, if you could read."

"I can read," said Townsend, pouting. "I can read all right. You don't need to work so hard at putting me down."

"It's not hard," said Myrtle. "Now are you going let Slocum out of there?"

"Oh, all right," said Townsend, picking up his keys. He walked over to the cell and unlocked the door. "Go on," he said to Slocum. "Get out of here."

"How about my Colt?" Slocum said.

"Oh," said Townsend, and he walked back to his desk, tossed down the keys, and opened the drawer. Taking out the Colt, he handed it to Slocum. Slocum dropped it in his holster. He turned to walk out of the office with Myrtle.

"Don't be so free with your threats from now on," said Townsend, trying to save face.

"I never threatened anyone," Slocum said. "Remember? It was just a simple question I asked. That's all."

Outside, Slocum and Myrtle walked toward the newspaper office. Slocum pulled the pad out of his pocket. He handed it to Myrtle.

"Here's what I found before I was interrupted," he said.

She took the pad and studied it, paying particular attention to the first page. She glanced up at Slocum. "You want a cup of coffee?" she asked.

"Sure."

They walked over to the eating place at the hotel and found a table. "Two coffees," Myrtle said when the waiter came over. She continued to look at the pad Slocum had handed her. "These first two names on here," she said, "I never even thought about them. It was still early. Thornton wasn't even a suspect yet. It's worse than I thought."

The waiter came back with the coffee. He set it down and left again.

"I think that's how come I got throwed in jail," Slocum said. "Somebody didn't want me checking into those land records too close."

"Somebody like Jobe Thornton," said Myrtle. "Elgin and Townsend are both kissing his ass. What more do you want?"

"I'd like some proof," Slocum said.

"Hell," said Myrtle, "I guess you're right. But how do we go about getting it?"

"I ain't right sure," said Slocum. "Let me keep working

on this. When we get all the information together that we can get, maybe it will be time enough then to publish it. Then we'll see if it's enough to make ole Thornton tip his hand."

"Maybe," she said. "But Slocum, there's got to be something else in this equation that we don't know about. Something bigger at stake. I've tried to figure out just why in hell Thornton would want this whole damn valley. I wouldn't take it if you was to give it to me. Thornton's Tall T Ranch is already as big as he needs. Bigger. He's got more money than this country has locoweed."

"If we could figure that out," Slocum said, "we might be more than halfway there. I don't suppose there's any gold around here?"

"Not a chance. Not that I ever heard."

"Silver?"

"Nope."

"Maybe ole Thornton just wants to be the biggest landowner in the history of the world."

Myrtle shook her head and took a sip of coffee. "I don't think so," she said.

"I don't either," said Slocum. "I'm just clutching at straws." He took a slurp of his coffee and put the cup down. "Maybe we don't need to know. Maybe just getting all that information together and publishing it will be enough to do the trick."

"Maybe," she said.

Townsend was back down the street at the land office. He was inside leaning across the counter at Elgin.

"I had to let him go," he said.

"How come?" said Elgin. "He threatened me."

"He didn't actually threaten you," said Townsend. "He just asked a simple question. That's all, and Myrtle was fixing to sue me."

"Well, damn."

"Elgin," said Townsend. "How much did he see?"

6

"Hell," said Elgin, "I don't know. I ran right out to fetch you back here."

"Damn it," said Townsend.

"He was taking notes, though," Elgin said. "He must've got the first few names."

"He can't do too much damage with just those. I don't think he can."

"Don't you think you'd ought to go out and tell Mr. Thornton about this?"

"Yeah. I guess so."

Myrtle had written down a list of names of settlers and small ranchers who had disappeared and whose property Jobe Thornton had wound up owning. She thought that it was pretty good evidence, but she knew what Mark Townsend would say if she presented it to him. The poor unfortunates had just dropped out of sight or been killed by drifters. With the property available, Thornton had just bought it up. That's all. She had no proof. No direct proof. All the evidence was circumstantial. Even Amos's attack on poor Sammy could be justified, sort of. The newspaper had been pretty hard on Thornton, and it could be said that Thornton, or his man Amos, had just been reacting to the bad publicity. Myrtle thought it was pretty telling that Sammy had been killed just after that too, but again, Townsend would say that there was no evidence.

She had just about decided that Slocum was probably right asking her to ease off for a spell. She knew, though, that Townsend was in Thornton's back pocket. Even with evidence, it would be a hell of a job getting Thornton into court on any serious charges. Somehow the evidence would have to be gotten into the hands of the judge without Thornton knowing anything about what was going on. She had an idea. Maybe she did not have enough evidence to take Thornton to court, but she thought that she did have enough evidence to call for a serious investigation. Townsend wasn't about to do it, but maybe the judge would, if he knew about it. She decided to let Slocum in on her thoughts, and just then he walked through the door.

"I been out talking to folks, Boss," he said.

"I wish you wouldn't call me that," Myrtle said.

"All right," he said, grinning. "I been out talking to folks, Myrtle. About half the ones I talked to agree with you about Thornton. The rest of them claim to not have any idea or any interest in what's going on."

"They're afraid to get involved," she said. "But listen to me. I've got an idea."

"All right," Slocum said. "Shoot."

"If we had a decent sheriff, do you think our evidence would be enough to call for an investigation?"

Slocum sat on the edge of a table and shoved back his hat. "I think so," he said, "but we don't have, so what's the use?"

"What if we could get that evidence to the judge?"

"That might not be a bad idea," he said. "It ought to at least get him thinking. And someone else ought to have the information anyhow, just in case."

"In case what?"

"Well, suppose something was to happen to me. Then it would be just you and your opinion. And I don't think you'd be any too safe all by yourself. Remember McGuire's wife."

"Could you get it to him, do you think?"

"What's his name and where do I find him?"

"Judge Ira Colter. He can be found over at the territorial capital, unless he's making the circuit. I don't know his schedule. It varies."

"I guess I'll take myself a long ride," Slocum said. "Now you be careful while I'm gone."

"I promise," she said. She handed Slocum the list of names she had compiled. Each name had a note beside it. It either said "Disappeared" or "Murdered," and then it said, "Property acquired by Jobe Thornton." The last name on the list was Sammy Sneed, and the note read, "Newspaper employee, beaten by Amos Dean, Thornton's hired man, and then murdered." A note at the bottom of the page read, "Sheriff Mark Townsend cannot be gotten interested in investigating." Slocum folded the paper and tucked it into his shirt while Myrtle hastily gathered up a few selected back issues of the *Beacon*. "Here," she said, "take him these too."

"All right," he said.

Slocum packed his roll and walked to the stable, where he paid Sam Black for looking after his big Appaloosa, saddled up, and climbed on.

"You leaving town?" Black asked.

"I'll be back," said Slocum.

"I'll keep a stall ready for you then," Black said, and he waved as Slocum headed out of town. Amos Dean was in the saloon having a drink. He watched out the window as Slocum rode out. He tossed down his drink and turned to face his two companions.

"Drink up, boys," he said. "We got work to do."

The three men went outside and mounted their horses. Amos started riding in Slocum's tracks. "Where we headed, Amos?" one of the two asked.

"We got us a man to kill," Amos said. "We'll go easy till we're well out of town. Then we'll speed up a little and catch up with him."

"One man?"

"He's all by hisself."

• • •

Sheriff Mark Townsend had ridden out to Thornton's Tall T Ranch, and Thornton had some coffee brought out to the front porch of the big ranch house. He and Townsend sat there at a large table. "What brings you out here, Mark?" Thornton asked.

"It's that Slocum," said Townsend. "He's gone to work for Myrtle at the paper, and he's already been snooping around."

"How snooping?" said Thornton.

"Elgin come into my office and told me that Slocum was down to his place snooping through the land records. He tried to keep him out of them, but Slocum threatened him, so he give him the record books and then come running after me. I put him in jail for threatening Elgin, but Myrtle said that what Slocum said wasn't really a threat, and she was going to sue me if I didn't turn him loose, so I did."

"Is that it?"

"Yes, sir, that's it. I thought you'd want to know about it, though."

"Yeah," said Thornton. "Yeah. Well, the land records ain't too important. The Gilligan woman already knows all that. Hell, she's published it in her goddamn paper. Just what did Slocum say to Elgin anyway?"

Townsend blushed a deep red. "He asked Elgin if he was going to have to get tough."

"It was pretty stupid of you to arrest him for that. Anyhow, what's most interesting of all you told me is that Slocum went to work for that woman. They're up to something. I wish the son of a bitch had taken my offer when I made it. I wonder where the hell Amos is at."

"Oh, he was in town at the saloon when I left to come out here," said Townsend. "Him and Leo Crutch and Slim Farley."

"Damn it," said Thornton. "Well, when you get back, send them right back out here."

"I'll do it, Mr. Thornton," said Townsend as he stood up to leave.

Slocum was riding the lonesome road that would eventually take him to the territorial capital when he thought that he could hear the sound of riders coming up behind him. He moved to the side of the road and dismounted just behind a large boulder and waited. Soon three riders came into his sight. In another minute, he recognized Amos. "Stand easy, big horse," he said as he moved to the other side of the boulder. The riders drew up quickly, surprised to find Slocum waiting for them there.

"Howdy," Slocum said. "It's Amos, ain't it? Who are your friends?"

Leo and Slim scowled in silence. Amos grinned.

"Yeah," he said. "You know it's Amos. And these here is Leo Crutch and Slim Farley. They ain't too bright, but they know how to shoot."

"We're bright enough," said Farley.

"Is this just a chance meeting," said Slocum, "or was it deliberate?"

"I seen you riding out of town," said Amos, "so I thought I'd ride out and catch up with you. Ask you a few questions."

"Like what?" said Slocum.

"Are you leaving town for good?"

"I could be."

"That would be real nice. I'd be glad to hear that."

"What else?"

"I been thinking about you since our last meeting," said Amos. "Slocum. Seems like I heard about you somewhere. You're supposed to be some kind of a gunfighter, ain't you? Are you that, Slocum?"

"My name's Slocum. I don't know what you've heard."

"I heard you killed Comstock and his whole outfit over to Hangtown all by your lonesome."

"You can hear a lot of things," said Slocum.

"What are we fooling around with him for?" asked Farley.

"You were right, Amos. They ain't too bright," said Slocum.

"They couldn't wipe their own ass without someone to tell then when and how," said Amos. "You mind if I get down?"

"Suit yourself."

"Wasn't no call for you to say that, Amos," said Crutch.

"Shut up," said Amos as he swung his leg over the horse's rump and stepped down onto the ground. He handed the reins to Farley and stepped away from the horse, facing Slocum. "The boss told me to leave you alone, Slocum."

"But you've got your own mind."

"That's right."

"And you mean to kill me."

"You got a better brain than both of these two put together."

"There he goes again, Slim," said Crutch.

Farley said, "Amos, you cut out talking like that about us. You hear?"

"Shut up," said Amos. "Boys, I want you to stay out of this unless he kills me."

Farley and Crutch looked at one another. Farley grinned. "Sure, Amos," he said.

"If you mean to kill me," said Slocum, "then you might not mind answering a few of my questions first."

"Why not?"

"It is you that's been killing off the small ranchers around here so Thornton can get their property, ain't it?"

Amos smiled a broad smile. "You recognize my style?" he asked.

"How come?"

"Now that ain't none of your business, Slocum."

"Humor me. Grant a dying man his last wish."

"Well," said Amos, "since you put it like that, a man

ought to know how come he's dying. Course, the real reason you're dying is on account of what you done to me in town."

"But what's behind it all?"

"The railroad's coming through, Slocum," said Amos. "Mr. Thornton wants all the land they're going to have to buy up for right-of-way, and time's getting short on him."

"So that's it."

"That's it. Now get ready to take a long trip. One you ain't coming back from."

Slocum eyeballed Amos and the other two men. He knew that Farley and Crutch weren't about to stay out of the fight. He figured that Amos would be the fastest of the three, but he thought that he could outdo Amos by a fair amount. He formulated a quick plan. Amos said, "Now!" Slocum drew and fired two quick shots, ducking behind the boulder. Farley and Crutch each had bullets in their chests. They each sat wobbling in their saddles with stupid looks on their faces. Each one dropped his gun and then slipped from the saddle, landing with a dull thud in the hard dirt below. It was so fast that it stunned Amos. His gun was only halfway out of its holster. He stopped still. He had turned to watch the other two drop dead, and when he looked back at Slocum, he saw the barrel of Slocum's Colt pointed straight at his gut.

"You going to go for it or not?" Slocum asked.

"Not like this," Amos said. "You got me killed already."

"Then unbuckle your gun belt and let it drop."

Amos hesitated only for an instant. Then he unbuckled the belt and let it fall to the road.

"What now?" he said.

"Back away from it," said Slocum. Amos backed away, and Slocum walked over to pick it up. He moved to his Appaloosa and tossed the gun belt across the horse's neck. Then he walked over to where the other two gunnies had dropped their six-guns, and he picked them up. He dropped them in his saddlebags. "Now," he said, "load those two up on their saddles."

Amos had to struggle a bit to get the two bodies up and slung across the saddles, but he got it done. Then he turned to face Slocum again.

"Tie the horses together. All three of them."

Amos again did as he was told, and Slocum fired another shot into the air, and slapped one of the horses on the ass. They whinnied and bolted and started to run.

"Hey," said Amos. "That one's my horse."

"Now you're getting smart," said Slocum. "Pull off your boots."

"What?"

"You heard me. Do it."

Amos tried pulling off one boot while still standing, but he fell over. He sat up in the dirt and pulled off both boots. "Get up," said Slocum. Amos stood. "Now get out of your britches."

"I ain't going to do that," said Amos.

"Then I'll just kill you," said Slocum, raising his Colt and cocking it.

"No. No. Wait," said Amos. "All right."

He got out of his trousers quickly and stood there in the road looking very foolish indeed. Slocum moved toward him, motioning him backward. As Amos stepped back, Slocum picked up the trousers and the boots. Then he walked back to his Appaloosa and mounted up.

"You going to leave me here like this?" Amos asked with a quaver in his voice.

"You ain't dead," said Slocum, and he started riding again toward the capital.

"Hey," shouted Amos. "Wait a minute. You can't do this to me. Come back here, you son of a bitch. I'll kill you for this. I'll kill you dead. Goddamn you. I'll shoot you in the back. You'll never know what happened. Goddamn it. Goddamn it."

He started after Slocum, but Slocum was already almost out of sight, and the rocks in the road hurt Amos's feet. He stood still for a moment staring after the lone figure on the road ahead. At last he turned around and started walking gingerly back toward Charlotte's Town and the Tall T Ranch just beyond. He did not know what he would do when he reached the town. He knew that he could not bring himself to walk into Charlotte's Town in his present condition. He would be a laughingstock, and he couldn't stand that. Goddamn Slocum to bloody hell.

7

Slocum was in the capital by the time Amos Dean reached the Tall T Ranch. Amos's feet were cut and blistered and bloody. He was hungry and thirsty, and he was about ready to cry or to kill or something. The first thing he did was go into the bunkhouse for some clothes. Then he limped back outside to the water trough and dipped out a bucket of water. Taking it with him back to the bunkhouse, he sat down and began soaking his pitiful feet. He was glad that no one else was in the bunkhouse at the time. After some minutes, he pulled his feet out and daubed at them with a towel. He wanted to go to the big house and see the boss, but he did not want to walk anymore, and he did not want to pull on his boots. He moaned and groaned and wailed there all by himself.

Slocum found Judge Ira Colter without any trouble at all. He was ushered into the judge's office by a pretty young secretary almost immediately after stepping into the waiting room. The judge was a big man, not fat, just brawny, with an ample and drooping mustache. The hair on top of his head was beginning to recede just a bit. When Slocum stepped into the office, Colter stood up and walked around his big desk to shake hands.

"What brings you here, Mr. Slocum?" he asked.

"I'd rather do without that 'mister,' " Slocum said. "Just call me Slocum."

"All right, Slocum," said the judge. "Now what can I do for you?"

"I come up from Charlotte's Town," Slocum said. "I'm working for Miss Myrtle Gilligan of the *Beacon*."

"Ah, yes, I know it well," said the judge.

"I ain't usually one to run to the law," Slocum said, "but this is a kind of special case, I guess. I was just riding through Charlotte's Town on my way to no place in particular. About the first thing I seen was a bully named Amos who works for Thornton knock down a harmless little fellow named Sneed who was selling papers on the street. Well, I made Amos pick up Sneed's papers and give them back to him. Right after that, someone killed Sneed down at the end of the street. Shot him from ambush. That's about when I took this job from Miss Myrtle. She told me that this Thornton has been killing folks and grabbing their land somehow. There's no proof, but there's a lot of what I guess you call circumstantial stuff. She sent me over here to see you with all this."

He pulled the papers out of his shirt and handed them to the judge. Colter thumbed through them. "It's going to take me a while to read through all this," he said. "Did you just ride in?"

"Yes, sir," said Slocum.

"Why don't you go have yourself a drink, something to eat maybe, while I read through it. Come back in a couple of hours. Give me time to soak it all in."

"All right," said Slocum. He walked out of the office and found the nearest saloon.

Back at the Tall T Ranch, Amos had finally gotten up the courage to pull on his boots. The pain was excruciating, and it took him about five minutes to get the job done. Then he couldn't bring himself to stand up. He sat there sucking in deep breaths and moaning. There was just one more problem, though, and that was that he was hungry as hell and he needed a drink. At last he hauled himself up and, wincing with pain, he managed to walk over to the cookshack.

"Egg," he called out, "bring me some grub and hurry it up."

"It ain't time," said Egg.

"I don't give a damn what time it is. Bring me some grub in a hurry, or I'll make you sorry you didn't."

Egg knew that Amos was a bad one, so with some grumbling, he set about putting a meal together. Finally, he tossed a plate of cold beef and biscuits on the table in front of Amos. As he did so, he noticed that Amos was looking pretty wretched. He also could see that Amos was unarmed. He had never seen Amos in such a state before. Oh, well, he told himself, it's best I do what he says on account of he'll likely recover from whatever it is ailing him. Amos was gnawing at a hunk of beef. "Get me a drink of whiskey," he said. Egg went to the cabinet and opened it. He took out a bottle and a glass and poured some whiskey into the glass. Then he set the glass down by Amos's plate. Amos grabbed it up and drank greedily. Just then the door burst open, and Thornton came striding into the room.

"Where the hell have you been, Amos?" he said. "I've had men looking all over for you."

"Well, you found me," said Amos, through his chewing.

"So where have you been?"

"Goddamn it, Thornton, I've been to hell and back, and I'm about to starve to death. Let me alone a while."

Thornton slapped the plate and glass off the table, smashing them against the wall. Amos jumped up, ready for a fight, but his reflexes were better off than was his beat-up body, and as soon as he stood, he winced in pain again and dropped back into the chair with a small cry of anguish. When Amos had jumped up, Thornton had noticed that he was unarmed. That emboldened him even more. "Now answer my goddamned question," he said.

"It was two days ago," said Amos. "Two long days and

nights. We was in town having a drink or two. Me and Farley and Crutch. We seen Slocum ride out of town. Well, I
know you told me to leave him alone, but I thought, hell, if
we was to catch him well enough out of town, no one
would be the wiser."

"That was about the time I told Townsend to look you
up and send you out here to me," said Thornton. "He said
he'd seen you three in town drinking. So you decided to
start in to thinking on your own, did you?"

"I didn't see no harm in it."

"All right. All right. Go on with the story."

"We caught up with him all right," said Amos. "But he
bushwhacked us. Killed Leo and Slim. Both of them. Dead-
er'n hell." He looked at the floor while told this little lie.

"How come he left you alive?"

"He's mean. That's how come. He chased my horse off.
Took my gun and my boots and my britches, and left me
out there like that. Left me to die with no way to defend
myself and no transportation. I didn't think I'd ever get
back here, walking like that, in my bare feet. They're cut
all to pieces. I didn't have no food, no water, no nothing. A
man ain't never been left in such dire straits. I can promise
you that."

"All right. Egg, give him another drink."

"And some more food," said Amos.

"Some more food," echoed Thornton. "I ought to be
mad as hell at you for going out on your own," he continued. "But the truth is, I sent for you to tell you to do exactly
what you done. Well, not exactly. But I was fixing to send
you after Slocum. Townsend told me that he caught
Slocum going through the land records in town."

"Oh," said Amos, glancing up at Thornton.

"Oh? Oh, what?"

"I guess he was kinda digging for the truth of what we
been up to around here. He asked me what was behind all
this, and I let it slip that the railroad was coming through."

"You goddamn fool," Thornton shouted. "You ass.
You—"

"Well, he had a gun on me. What could I do?"

"I ought to kill you myself."

"Take it easy, Boss. You wasn't there. You don't know what it was like."

"Men have gone to their deaths before betraying a secret like that."

"Well, I thought that he was going to be dead. I didn't think he would ever live to be around and repeat it to no one. I—"

Amos suddenly stopped talking, realizing that he had betrayed himself. He hoped that Thornton hadn't noticed, but he was wrong.

"Wait a minute," said Thornton. "You said that Slocum bushwhacked you. How is it that when you was talking to him, you thought that he was going to be dead?"

"Well, um, you see, he'd done killed Leo and Slim, and he had the drop on me, but then he holstered his gun and told me to draw on him, you know, like a gunfighter will do sometimes, and I thought that I'd beat him to the draw and kill him. That's when I told him. But then he drawed on me so fast that I never had a chance. He's fast, Boss. I never seen anyone so fast."

"That sounds like so much bullshit to me," said Thornton. "But never mind that now. Slocum had been into the land records, and he was leaving town. Which way did he ride out?"

"He was on the road to the capital."

"Damn it. He might be going to see the judge with those records. He might—"

"He said he was just leaving town—for good."

"And you fell for that?"

"Well—"

"We can't let him get back here. You get some of the boys and get back out on that road. Lay in an ambush, and this time kill him."

"I can't go, Boss. I need to lay up for a few days and recover from my serious wounds."

"You'll go all right, I want you to make up for the fool thing you already done."

•   •   •

Slocum was back at Judge Colter's office. He took a seat across from the judge at the big desk. Colter hefted the papers that Slocum had delivered to him. He dropped them back on the desk. "This is real interesting reading, Slocum," he said. "Real interesting."

"I know we got no real proof, Judge," Slocum said. "But I did discover a reason behind it all. On my way here, three rannies from the Tall T tried to ambush me, but I turned the table on them. I killed two of them, but not before the leader bragged a while and then admitted that Thornton wants to grab up all the land for the railroad right-of-way. No one around Charlotte's Town even knows about the railroad yet."

"And the land that Thornton has been grabbing up—"

"Is all in the railroad's path," Slocum said.

"That figures," said the judge. "Well, you may not have any solid evidence, but you damn sure have enough here to call for an investigation. Has Sheriff Townsend over there been investigating this any at all?"

"Far as we can tell, Judge, he's in Thornton's pocket."

"Well, that's no big surprise. Tell you what I'm going to do, Slocum. I'm going to ride back to Charlotte's Town with you. It's late, so we'll leave first thing in the morning. Right now, I'll walk you over to the hotel and buy you a supper. I'll get you a room at the territory's expense."

Standing up, the judge picked up the stack of papers Slocum had brought. He stuffed them into a satchel and, carrying them with him, walked out the door. Slocum followed. In the waiting room, the receptionist stood up. "Are you ready, Ira?" she said.

"Yes, my dear," Colter said. "Oh, Slocum, I guess you've already met my wife, Corrine?"

Slocum flushed slightly. He had been thinking naughty thoughts about the lovely young thing. He took off his hat. "Well, no, not exactly," he said. "Pleased to meet you, ma'am."

"Likewise, Mr. Slocum," she said.

"Come along, my dear," said Colter. "We're going to walk Mr.—uh, we're going to walk Slocum to the hotel and have a meal with him. I'll tell you all about it along the way."

At the hotel restaurant, they ordered steak dinners and had a leisurely meal. Slocum had a few glasses of whiskey with his. He had trouble keeping his eyes off the judge's young wife. Colter explained to his wife that he would be leaving town for a few days with Slocum to investigate the goings-on around Charlotte's Town. She whined and whimpered that she would miss him terribly while he was gone, and he simpered back to her that he would miss her just as much but that his duty called. Slocum thought that he would be sick to his stomach if it went on much longer. He had another whiskey. In a bit, the judge paid for the meal and went to the hotel desk, where he charged a room for Slocum. Slocum took the key and thanked the judge. They all walked back out onto the street. The sun was low in the west.

"Well, good night, Slocum," said the judge. "I'll see you at sunup down at the livery ready to ride."

Slocum tipped his hat to Mrs. Colter and watched them walk away arm in arm. Then he got his stallion and rode him to the livery stable. Taking his bedroll, he walked back to the hotel.

Amos Dean rearmed himself out of the arsenal of the Tall T Ranch and groaned and cried all the way to a horse in the Tall T corral. He yelled at a ranch hand and made him catch the horse and saddle it up for him. "I'm crippled up too bad," he said. Five other gunhands mounted up to ride along with Amos. Amos was grumbling at the utter cruelty of Thornton in making him ride out again so soon after his misfortune. He thought that he really needed several days of recovery before going out to work again. When the horse was brought to him, saddled and ready to go, Amos took the reins and grabbed hold of the horn. He put his foot into the stirrup and started to mount, but the pressure on his foot hurt too bad. "Help me up," he said, and the cowhand who had saddled the horse put hands on Amos's butt and shoved. With a yelp, Amos swung up into the saddle. He sat there for a moment breathing deeply, recovering from the pain. Then he said, "All right, boys, let's ride."

Amos led the way, almost crying from the pain. It was not just that his feet were in such a mess from all the bare-footed walking he had done. It was more than that. Every muscle in his body ached. He was not a man used to walking. And he had walked for two days. Each step the horse took sent shooting pangs of misery through his muscles and bones all the way to his head. He tried to think of the intense pleasure he would derive from seeing Slocum shot to pieces, but even that did not work. The pain was just too much. And he would not get to watch Slocum suffer. He would have to tell the men to just shoot and keep shooting until Slocum was a bloody piece of meat lying in the road. He could not take any chances this time. Slocum had to be killed. He did not think that Slocum would be traveling at night, but he couldn't take a chance there either. He had to be sure. "Buber," he called out.

A gunman rode forward to his side. "Yeah, Amos?"

"Buber, I want you to ride ahead. Slocum don't know you, does he?"

"I don't think so," said Buber.

"Good. You ride ahead, and if you pass him on the road, just keep on a-going. When you get past him a ways, ride off the road and come back to tell us. I don't think he'll be riding tonight, but you just never know."

"What if I get all the way to the capital and never see him?"

"Then see if you can find out anything and turn around and come back to find us."

"How'll I find you?"

"We'll see you coming down the road."

Buber rode on out, and the rest crept along in his wake. The road dropped down a bit, and Amos felt like it had dropped out from under him. He moaned out loud. Someone behind him called out, "You all right, Amos?"

"Hell, no," Amos answered, "but never mind."

He rode on a bit farther, and the road rose up again, and again Amos cried out in pain at the change in the horse's gait. At long last, well into the night, they came to the place that Amos had in mind. The side of the road to his left rose up a hillside that was covered in large rocks. There was a sort of a trail winding between the rocks to the top of the hill, and Amos led the way up the miserable trail, whining and cursing his horse with every step. At last they were all on top. Amos had the men lead the horses down the other side of the hill and tether them there. Then he placed each man strategically behind boulders where each man had a good view of the road below and a clear shot at anything that came riding along. He nestled himself down in his own spot with his rifle across his knees. He was feeling mighty sorry for himself, but at last he began to really think of the pleasure the sight of Slocum's bloody corpse would give him, and he actually smiled.

8

Slocum went back to the bar and had another couple of drinks. Then he went on up to his room and got himself ready for bed. Lying on top of the covers, he thought about the ride back to Charlotte's Town. He wondered what would come next. There was no way of knowing. He was a careful man, never quite trusting anyone until he knew for sure, and he did not really know Judge Colter. He thought that the man was all right, but he wasn't sure. Did Colter know Thornton? If so, how well did he know him? Myrtle trusted the judge, and that was almost enough for Slocum. Almost. Then he wondered about Amos. It occurred to him that he would have been really smart to kill the son of a bitch. But he hadn't needed to kill Amos, and so he had not killed him. He had left him in a difficult position to be sure, but he had left him alive. If Amos had managed to get himself back to the Tall T, he would be mad as hell and aching for revenge. And if he, or Thornton, had figured out what Slocum was up to, they just might see it as a golden opportunity to lay an ambush for him along the road for his return trip. They might. He would have to be on the lookout for that.

• • •

Ira Colter walked his wife home. Inside, she packed a bag for him while he got out his two pearl-handled Colt revolvers and checked them over. They were in good working order, well oiled. He loaded them and checked his gun belt, which was full of extra shells. He got out another box of shells and dropped them in his coat pocket. He looked over at his wife as she fastened his bag.

"Everything's ready," he said. "I'll be riding out at daybreak."

"Yes, I know," she said.

Ira Colter took the bag and the gun belt to the front door. He placed the bag by the door and hung the rig up on a peg beside the door. Then he took off his jacket and hung it up there too. His hat was already perched by the door. He turned and saw Corrine standing expectantly in the bedroom doorway. Light from the street came through the window shade behind her and gave her an unearthly, angelic glow. He was overcome with intense feelings of passionate desire. He walked toward her smiling, and as he approached, she held out her arms. He walked into them, and they closed around his shoulders. Their lips met in a tender kiss that grew passionate in a short time. Suddenly, Colter swept Corrine up into his arms and carried her to the bed. He tossed her onto the mattress and standing over her, began to strip off his clothes. She lay there watching him, writhing suggestively. At last he was stark naked, his manly rod standing out ready for action, bouncing up and down in anticipation of the joy to come. Colter crawled in the bed on top of Corrine. He lay down on her and began smothering her with kisses.

"Oh, Ira," she moaned.

Then he began fumbling with her clothing, unfastening things here and there, pulling pieces of it off her and tossing them aside onto the floor. He was panting in his anxiety to get on with it, and Corrine panted in response. At last he had her stripped, and he laid his weight back on top of her and kissed her some more. He kissed her mouth and her eyes, and he nuzzled into her neck. He eased himself down a bit and began sucking at her gorgeous nipples. They stood out hard the more he slurped.

"Oh, Ira," she moaned. "Oh, I love what you do to me."

"Yes. Yes," he said, and he eased himself down further, kissing her smooth belly, tonguing her tiny belly button, and at last reaching her special, precious, damp and curling pubic hair. He nuzzled her pussy with his nose and shot out his sharp tongue, which began to lick the insides of her cunt lips.

"Oh, Ira," she said. "More. More."

Colter shoved his tongue deep into her hungry cavern and lapped and licked and slurped until she cried out for mercy, and then he crawled back up her now sweaty body and slathered her lips with his wide-open mouth. She tasted her own juices mingled with his saliva.

"Here. Here," she said. "Let me."

She shoved him to one side, and he rolled over onto his back. Corrine wasted no time. She moved quickly to his cock, still stiff, and grasped it hard. It jumped in her grip as if it wanted to break loose, but she clamped her lips over it. She lolled it around in her mouth. She licked it around and around, and then suddenly she slurped its entire length into her mouth. Colter gasped out loud as if he had been doused with a bucket of cold water. Then he began humping and thrusting upward, moving in and out of her mouth. Corrine's head moved up and down in rhythm with his strokes.

"Um, um, um," she moaned.

"Oh, oh, oh," he said.

Their pace quickened, and at last Colter said, "Oh, I'm going to—Oh, oh."

"Um?" she said. It was all she could manage with her mouth so full.

Then Colter felt the pressure build. And then it exploded, shooting burst after burst of hot cum juice into the waiting mouth of Corrine. She slurped and sucked, swallowing great loads. At last Colter lay still panting. Corrine slipped the cock out of her mouth and held it in her hands and fondled it as it went limp. Then she crawled up to lay her head on his chest and nestle in his arms for a good night's sleep. It had been a lovely session. She did not know how long it would have to last them.

Slocum was at the livery strapping his bedroll on behind the saddle when Colter rode up the following morning. The judge sat in the saddle, his six-guns strapped on around his waist and his valise tied to the saddle. "Had your breakfast?" he asked.

"I just got up," said Slocum.

"Well, finish up there, and we'll ride down to Judy's place for a bite to eat."

Slocum finished and mounted, and the judge led the way. Just outside of town, they stopped at a small house beside the road. A sign out front read JUDY'S PLACE. They dismounted and went inside. It had the look of a home with its front room made over into an eatery. It was early in the morning, and no one else was in yet. The judge took a seat at the first table inside the door. Slocum sat down opposite him. In a moment, a fine-looking young woman appeared. She was wearing an apron and wiping her hands on a towel. Strands of her brown hair hung down in her face, giving her a slightly disheveled but still attractive appearance. She smiled when she saw the judge. He smiled back, a broad smile.

"Ham and eggs and potatoes," he said. "And coffee. You're looking at two hungry men, Judy."

Judy looked at Slocum. "And for you?"

"The same," he said.

"Coming right up." Judy disappeared through a door, and came back a moment later with two cups of coffee, which she put on the table.

"Judy," said the judge, "this is Slocum. I'm riding down to Charlotte's Town with him on business."

"Hello, Slocum," said Judy.

Slocum took off his hat. "Howdy, ma'am," he said.

"I'll have your breakfasts out in a jiffy," she said, and she disappeared again.

"A fine woman," said the judge.

"Mighty fine-looking," said Slocum.

The judge then passed the time asking Slocum more questions about Charlotte's Town and the things that had been going on, and he asked about Myrtle and how she was doing. Slocum answered the questions as best he could, and then Judy brought out the plates. There was no more talk then. As they ate, a couple more customers came in. Their meals finished, Slocum and the judge drank an extra cup of coffee each, and got up to leave. The judge paid for the food, and Slocum caught a look that Colter gave to Judy just before they went outside. There was something in that look, something more than just friendly. They mounted up and started their long ride.

Amos had sat stiffly behind his rock all night long, and he was beginning to hurt worse than ever. The sun was coming up, and Buber had not yet returned. He decided that meant that Slocum was not yet near them and he could stand up and move around a bit. With a moan, he got himself to his feet, and the pain shot up through his body again. Still, he needed the movement. He staggered a few steps on the uneven ground. "Boys," he called out, "get up and move around a bit. I think we got some time yet. Ow. Oh."

The man nearest him took a few steps in his direction. "You all right, Amos?"

"Hell, no," said Amos. "I'm a long ways from all right, but that don't make no difference to ole Thornton. The cold-blooded son of a bitch. Listen, Cowlick, you think you could build up a pot of coffee? I don't think that Slocum is anywhere near yet, and I could sure use some coffee."

"Sure, Amos, I can do that. Where you want me to put the fire?"

Amos turned around, a groan accompanying each small step, and pointed toward the top of the hill to a small out-cropping of rocks. "Right up there," he said. Cowlick started toward the outcropping.

Ahead on the road, Buber was riding along alone. He had not seen anyone. He had ridden all night, and he was beginning to feel hungry. He thought about coffee, and he began to crave some. He wondered if he had been sent on a wild-goose chase. Where was that Slocum anyway? He decided that if he made it all the way to the capital, he would not worry about Slocum. He would just find a place to eat and drink coffee and to hell with Slocum. Let Amos worry about Slocum. Goddamn it.

At about noon, Slocum and Colter stopped to prepare a meal. They built a small fire beside the road. They had some beans from a tin, some cold biscuits, and a pot of coffee. All of this had been packed for the judge by his young wife. They were sitting and eating when a rider came down the road from the direction of Charlotte's Town. The rider approached cautiously. When he came near, the judge called out to him. "Come on into the camp, stranger."

The man rode in and dismounted. "Much obliged," he said.

"You hungry?" the judge asked.

"Sure am."

Colter handed the man a plate of beans and a biscuit. The man began eating as if he had not eaten in days. Colter poured a cup of coffee and gave it to the man. "You coming from Charlotte's Town?" he asked.

The man looked up at the judge and swallowed. Then he sipped some coffee. "Rode through there," he said.

Something in the man's look made Slocum suspicious. "Just rode through?" he asked.

"Yeah. That's all."

Slocum sipped his coffee, but he held the cup in his left hand, keeping his right near his Colt.

"What about you fellows?" the man asked. "Headed for Charlotte's Town?"

"That's right," said the judge. "On business."

"My name's Cord Buber," the man said. "Didn't catch yours."

"We didn't throw them," said Slocum.

"I'm Judge Colter."

Buber's eyes widened. He knew that the other man was Slocum, but what was Slocum doing riding with a judge? This did not bode well, he thought. He finished his meal and slurped down the rest of his coffee. Then he stood up and headed for his horse.

"Well," he said, "I better be moving on. Thanks for your hospitality."

Buber mounted his horse and headed back to the road. He angled the animal in the direction of the capital and moved on at an easy pace. He did not want to cause Slocum and the judge to have any suspicions. He did not look back, although it was a strain to keep from doing so. Back at the campsite, Slocum watched the man as he rode on.

"What's the matter, Slocum?" asked Judge Colter. "You know that man?"

"Don't know him," Slocum said, "but I don't like him."

"Why not?"

"There's just something about him," Slocum said. "Something about the way he looked when you named yourself a judge, and then he sure was in a hurry to get away."

"He rode away leisurely enough," said Colter, "and he rode in the wrong direction to be of any danger to us."

"Yeah? We'll see."

They put out the fire and packed the pots away. When they mounted up to ride, Slocum said, "You ride on ahead. I'll catch up with you in a bit."

"What are you up to?"

"I just want to check something out," said Slocum, and he kicked his big Appaloosa into a run. Colter shrugged and rode ahead. Slocum rode far enough to be sure that he had lost Buber. There was a long stretch of road ahead, and the way Buber had been riding, Slocum should have been able to see him up there, but he could not. That meant only one thing. Buber had left the road. Slocum studied the tracks in the road, but he couldn't tell anything from them. He turned and headed back toward Charlotte's Town, but he watched the side of the road till he saw a place where it was easy to ride off to the left. He moved off that way slowly. To his left, which was back toward Charlotte's Town, the ground rose into a low and rocky hill. He moved toward it, and when he reached it, he started riding up toward the top. It wasn't high here, but he recalled that some distance on down it rose somewhat higher. He moved up onto the ridge and squinted ahead, and there he saw Buber riding hard on the flat plain off to his right. He turned around and made his way back down the hill and back out to the road. Then he kicked up his stallion and hurried to catch up with the judge.

When Colter heard the fast hoofbeats coming up behind him, he turned and looked over his shoulder. He relaxed when he saw that it was Slocum. Slocum slowed down when he came up beside Colter. The judge said, "Well, what did you find out?"

"I think they're laying for us up ahead," Slocum said. "That Buber, if that was his name, moved off the road back there and did a right about. He's moving pretty fast back towards Charlotte's Town, but he's moving off over there on the other side of the hill."

"You mean that someone's laid an ambush, and they sent him ahead to scout us out?"

"That's what it looks like to me."

"What do you suggest we do?"

"Turn around."

"Turn around and go back?" said Colter.

"Turn around and follow Buber. They'll be watching for us on the road."

Colter grinned. "An admirable plan," he said, and the two men turned their mounts. Slocum led the way back to where he had left the road. Then they rode the flat plain behind the hill, the same way Buber had ridden. They were in no hurry, but they watched ahead carefully for any signs of Buber or of his companions. By nightfall, they had seen nothing. They decided to sleep in a cold camp and move out again in the morning.

Back in his hiding place, Amos was getting fed up. He decided that Slocum was not coming back at all. He had left town, the way he said he was doing. Amos did not intend to camp out on this hillside for days waiting for someone to show up who was long gone out of the territory, especially in the shape he was in. He thought about quitting Thornton and riding out himself, but then he remembered all the money Thornton was going to make when the railroad came through Charlotte's Town and the valley it was nestled in. He wanted his share of that money. He decided he would wait until morning. He would wait for Buber to return. He would wait a little while longer.

9

Slocum and the judge were up before the sun. They decided to move right on and worry about their bellies later. There was a damn good chance that an ambush was laid for them up ahead, and they did not want to give anyone a warning by lighting a fire. Cold biscuits without coffee did not sound very appetizing to either one of the two men. They rolled up their blankets, saddled the horses, and tied the rolls on behind the saddles. Then they mounted up to ride. They had ridden for a couple of hours before their guts began complaining so much that they went ahead and ate a couple of cold biscuits while they rode along. They washed the sorry breakfast down with tepid water from their canteens. Then Slocum decided to go up on the rise again for another look around. When he made it to the top, he saw a thin plume of smoke up ahead. He moved back down to rejoin Colter.

"I seen smoke from a campfire up ahead," he said.

"You suppose the damn fools have been fixing themselves a meal?" asked the judge.

"Or just having themselves a cup of morning coffee," said Slocum.

"If they're that stupid," the judge said, "they shouldn't be too hard to get evidence on. What do we do now?"

"Let's keep on riding back here behind the hills," Slocum said. "If they're laying for us on the road, they'd have hid their horses somewhere. I can't think of any place to hide horses except on this backside of these hills. We ought to spot them before they know we're coming."

"Sounds good to me."

They moved ahead with caution. In a short while, they could see the plume of smoke from where they were riding.

"Looks to me to be another two—three hours ride," Colter said.

"That's about what I make it," said Slocum.

Ahead, on the other side of the hill, Amos sat drinking a cup of coffee, still moaning because of his sore feet and muscles. He was beginning to be impatient. He did not believe that Slocum was coming back to Charlotte's Town at all. The son of a bitch had simply run out because of the odds against him. He knew too that Amos would be laying for him to get his revenge. For all Slocum knew, someone had come along and rescued Amos, and he was still in good shape. That was all there was to it. The son of a bitch had run out. Amos decided that he would wait for the return of Buber, if that bastard hadn't run out on him. Buber could be at the capital by now laid up with a couple of whores and a bottle of good whiskey. He was just the type to do that, run out on his buddies when things went to getting tough. Amos almost felt like riding ahead to find the little weasel and kill him. Then he heard some voices behind him, and he turned with a groan to see who was talking. Buber was angling down the hillside between the big rocks. Some of the others were greeting him.

"What'd you find?" said Amos, his voice betraying his impatience.

"They're coming all right," said Buber. He huffed and puffed as he struggled along the last few feet to where Amos was secreted.

"They? Who the fuck is they?" said Amos.

"That Slocum feller and the judge."

"Judge?"

"That Judge Colter from the capital."

"Riding together? Them two?"

"That's right. I rode right into their camp. I eat with them and drunk their coffee. The judge interduced himself to me and said they was riding to Charlotte's Town on business."

"What kind of business?"

"He never said that. Anyhow, soon as I was finished eating, I got out of there. I didn't let them see me turn around. I made out like I was headed for the capital, and when I got out of sight of them, I swung off the road and come along behind the hills."

"Good thinking," said Amos. "How far back are they?"

"Well," said Buber, "I figger if they got going at daylight this morning, they'd ought be riding along down there long about noon."

Amos stood up and called his gang together. "Slocum's a-coming," he said, "and he's got Judge Colter with him. We're going to have to kill the both of them now. Get that fire doused and settle back down to watch. Buber figgers they won't be here till noon, but we ain't taking no chances. Get on now."

"Where do you want me, Amos?" said Buber.

"Like I said, we ain't taking no chances. I want you to go over to the other side of the hill and hide yourself real good and watch our horses. They might come along that way, but I doubt it. Even so, watch real good. If you see them, start in to shooting, and shoot to kill. If we hear your shots, we'll hustle on up there to give you a hand."

Buber stood up again and started scampering up the hillside. Amos got excited. He was anxious to see the dead body of Slocum.

Randal and Tildy Morgan drove into Charlotte's Town with a wagon load of kids. It was time to stock up on provisions, and Tildy had said that the poor McGuire kids, Georgie and Bonnie, needed some new duds. Money was scarce, but Randal did not argue. He had lived with Tildy long enough to know better than that. Besides, he agreed with her. He had known the McGuire kids' parents, and he had liked them, but it was more than that. He had taken to the kids quite a lot. He was beginning to feel almost as if they were his own. Little Bonnie was always trying to help Tildy around the house, and outside, Georgie was a big help to Randal. They were good kids, but there was a brooding about them, which was, of course, understandable. The poor little tykes had witnessed the murders of their parents. That had to have been an awful thing for them.

Randal pulled up in front of Slats O'Toole's General Store. As he set the brake on the wagon, Myrtle Gilligan came walking up. "Howdy, Myrtle," Randal said.

"Hello, Randal. Tildy. And how are all the kids?"

"Fine," the children murmured.

From the front window in Thornton's real-estate office across the street, Jobe Thornton stood and watched. He could not hear anything, but he was concerned that the newspaper woman was talking to the Morgans, and that the two McGuire brats were there in the wagon. Amos should have seen to the brats. Thornton was beginning to think that it was about time he found a way to get rid of Amos. He had gotten too careless of late. He had let the McGuire brats get away, and he had let Slocum get away from him once. Killing that harmless newspaper seller had been foolish too. He would have to get rid of Amos—some way.

As the Morgans and the two McGuires got out of the wagon out on the street, Myrtle said, "Randal, when you're all through with your shopping, why don't you stop by my office for some coffee—and some candy for the children?"

The eyes of all the kids lit up a bit at that, and Randal glanced at Tildy, who smiled and nodded. Randal said, "Sure thing, missy."

The sun was almost straight overhead, and Amos and his bunch were getting ready, their palms sweating and their heartbeats going a bit faster than usual. On the backside of the hill, Buber sat tense. Just down the way from him, but not yet in his sight, Slocum and Colter rode along slowly. Ahead, the line of hills curved slightly to their left, and Slocum caught a glimpse of a horse's ass. "Hold it, Judge," he said. "Look up there."

"I see it," said Colter.

"Let's move on ahead just a little more," said Slocum, and they rode slowly on until they could see that several horses were picketed there.

"It's just like you called it," Colter said. "They're all laid out on the other side of the hills waiting for us to come along on the road."

"They might not be *all* laid out over there," Slocum said.

"What do you mean?"

"They might have one or two laying back here. That one that we fed last night has for sure got back to let them know we're coming, and it might have soaked into some thick skull that we could have followed him back here."

"You're right. I suggest that we dismount right here, climb up on top, and approach them on foot."

"Just what I was thinking, Judge."

They left their horses and started climbing. It was not a rough climb, but Slocum was a bit surprised at the agility of the judge, who moved up between the rocks with the ease of a cat. Just before they reached the top, they started moving toward the outlaws. They moved slowly, cautiously, from the cover of one rock to another. It was all of twenty minutes before Colter spotted the glint of a rifle barrel poking out from behind a boulder ahead. He reached over to tap Slocum on the shoulder and gestured toward the glint. Slocum looked, saw it, and nodded. He eased his Colt out of its holster and moved ahead, careful to make as little noise as possible. Judge Colter unholstered one of his Colts. They moved in a little closer, and then they could see Buber, watching down below. He was parked on the hillside close to the top just above the horses. They moved in more, and then Colter said, "Don't make a move, friend. Drop your rifle and stand up."

Buber's head jerked around. His eyes were wide and his mouth dropped open. He turned and stood quickly with a little cry, and he swung the rifle around to fire, but the judge's Colt blasted first, and the slug tore into Buber's chest. "Ak," he gurgled. He stood for a moment, a stupid look on his face. His head tipped forward as he looked down at the splotch of blood on his shirtfront. He looked up again in the direction of his killer, but his eyes were blank and staring, seeing nothing. His hands relaxed and let the rifle fall, and then his lifeless body pitched forward and landed hard on the rocks.

"Good shooting, Judge," said Slocum.

"A lucky shot," said the judge.

"They'll be coming now," Slocum said.

"Let them roar," said Colter.

The one called Cowlick was the first to appear on top of the hill, and Colter dropped him with a second shot. Then another appeared, and Slocum snapped off a round that took the hat off the man's head. The man ducked back down out of sight.

"Hell," said Slocum. "You're doing a lot better than I am."

"Just lucky," said Colter. "I wonder how many are over there."

"No way to tell," said Slocum. "We're in a Mexican standoff now."

"Let's crawl on ahead a ways," said the judge, "and go over the top on the other side of them."

"It's the best idea I've heard yet," said Slocum, and they started to move. As they did, they each reloaded their Colts. Slocum grumbled to himself because he had only one spent bullet to replace, and that one had done no good.

On the other side of the hill, someone called out to Amos. "What are we going to do? If we go up on top, they'll pick us off."

"Shut up," said Amos. "I'm thinking. Just keep watching up there."

Amos was wishing that he had left the horses on this side of the hill. He had a powerful urge to mount up and ride off to safety, but Slocum and the judge were between him and the mounts. Goddamn it, he thought. They done got two of my men. There's just four of us now against them two. He did not like the odds. He decided that if they just sat still, stayed hunkered down, the two on the other side would have to come over the top sooner or later. He decided that he could wait them out. Let them show their heads first, and then we'll blow them off. That's what they done to my boys, he thought. Well, that could work two ways. He would just wait it out. Several minutes passed. "Amos," said one in a harsh whisper. "Amos."

"What?" Amos answered in the same manner.

"You reckon they've took off?"

"You wanta poke your fool head up there and find out?"

There was no answer. Amos's feet began to plague him once again. He turned slightly to get a better angle on the hilltop, and pain shot through his muscles. Goddamn that fucking Slocum anyway.

Colter stopped crawling and looked back at Slocum. The outlaws' horses down below were well behind them. The judge gave a quizzical look, then looked up toward the top of the hill, and Slocum nodded. They inched their way up. Colter reached the top ahead of Slocum. He did not stand. Instead, he crawled up on his belly. No one fired. He saw no one stand up. He could see no one concealed. Slocum crept up after him. They looked at one another questioning. Colter gave a shrug. It seemed that they were not much better off than they had been before. It was still a matter of who decided to show himself first, and that one was liable to get plugged. Then Slocum noticed a large rock poised precariously on the side of the hill. He calculated that if it started to roll, it would be on this side of Amos and his bunch and not do them any damage, but it might just startle them into revealing themselves. He looked back at the judge and pointed to the rock. Then he made a motion as if the rock were going over the edge. The judge grinned and nodded his head. Slocum began inching toward the rock. When he got close enough, he turned himself around and put both feet against it. He shoved. The rocked budged a little, but that was all. It was a tougher job than he had figured. Colter inched over and joined Slocum. With four feet pushing, the rock tilted. It rocked back in place, and they shoved again. This time it rolled forward, balancing like an overweight dancer on toe shoes, and then it rolled forward. There was a loud crunching sound followed by grinding and scratching, and then a rumble as the rock picked up steam and other rocks and a slide was under way. Dust rose up in thick clouds. They could hear surprised shouting through the thick dust.

"Look out," someone shouted.

"Goddamn it."

"Rock slide."

Slocum and the judge got to their feet, Slocum with his Colt out, the judge with a Colt in each hand. They squinted through the dust. They ran forward on top of the hill. Then they saw one figure rising up from behind a rock. No one shouted a warning. Slocum fired, and the man dropped. Wild shots came through the dust cloud, none coming close to either Slocum or the judge. Colter fired another shot, and another outlaw bit the dust. Then Slocum fired again and dropped yet another.

Amos was still huddled down behind his boulder. At last he figured out that the rock slide was not coming at him. He could hear no more shots. There were only two of them up there, he thought. Perhaps he could pick them off. But he had to twist his body around. He started to do that, but it hurt him too bad. He would have to quit. Give it up. He hated the thought. He remembered what Slocum had done to him before, but he thought that since Slocum was in the company of a judge, he wouldn't be able to do that again.

Slocum would have to just take him in to jail. With Townsend in charge of the jail and Thornton's money behind him, Amos ought to be able to get out easily enough. He tossed his rifle away and ducked down again, just in case.

"Don't shoot no more," he shouted out. "I give up. That was my rifle you heard a clattering on the rocks. Don't shoot. Here comes my six-gun. Don't shoot."

He pulled the six-gun out and tossed it over the rocks.

"Stand up with your hands high," said Colter.

"All right. All right."

Amos stood, groaning all the way, and lifted his hands high over his head. "Don't shoot," he said.

10

Randy and Tildy Morgan were in Myrtle's office with all the kids, Georgie and Bonnie McGuire, and all three Morgan children, little Randy, Bobby, and Marty, the little girl. Myrtle got everyone seated comfortably and offered a bowl of hard candy to the children. They each took a chunk, and shoved them in their mouths eagerly.

"Thank you, ma'am," said Georgie McGuire. The others all took his cue and gave their thanks as well.

"You're welcome, children," said Myrtle, and she poured three cups of coffee for the adults, herself included. She passed cups to the Morgans, took one for herself, and sat down. "How are you doing with the children?" she asked.

"We're doing all right," said Tildy. "Georgie and Bonnie are good kids. Well mannered. They both of them help us out a lot."

"It's a little hard now with five of them, but we're managing," said Randy.

"I'd like to help," said Myrtle. She stood up and, taking some folded up bills out of her pocket, handed them to Tildy.

"You don't have to do that, Miz Gilligan," Tildy said.

"We ain't charity cases, ma'am," said Randy.

"You may not be," said Myrtle, "but Georgie and Bonnie are, and you don't have to shoulder the entire burden alone."

"Well . . ." Tildy murmured.

"Since you put it like that," said Randy, "well, okay."

"It's mighty kind of you," said Tildy. "We thank you."

"Is anybody gonna get that man?" asked Georgie.

The room suddenly grew quiet. Everyone knew what man Georgie was referring to, and no one knew quite what to say. Myrtle at last broke the silence. "We're working very hard at it, Georgie," she said. "We'll get him. Don't you worry."

"I think about him at nighttime," Georgie said. "It's hard to sleep."

"It's best to let the grownups do the worrying about that scoundrel," said Randy. "You just try to put it out of your mind. You're too young to worry about such things."

"I can't put it out of my mind," Georgie said. "I think about it all the time."

"Me too," said Bonnie.

Tildy reached out for Bonnie, who ran to her and sat in her lap, snuggling against her breast and shoulder, still sucking on her piece of hard candy.

"I see him plain in my mind," Georgie said.

Myrtle suddenly had an idea. "Georgie," she said, "can you draw pictures?"

"I use to draw if we ever had any extra paper in the house. Ma and Pa said I could draw real good."

"Come over here, Georgie," said Myrtle. "Come with me."

Georgie followed Myrtle to a long table, which was piled up with paper and ink trays and pieces of type. Myrtle shoved some of it aside, creating a clear place to work, and she laid out a piece of paper. Then she got a pencil and handed it to Georgie. "Draw him for me," she said. Georgie took the pencil and looked up into Myrtle's eyes. They were intense. They held him for a moment. Georgie's face was grim. He looked down at the blank paper, and then he started to draw. First an oval for a head. Then a black hat perched on top. Then a torso and arms and legs. He shaded the shirt black, and he put a gun in the man's hand. Then he went to work on the facial features. It was the work of a child, but it was pretty good, and as soon as he was done, Myrtle said, "Amos Dean."

As soon as the Morgan family, with its new additions, was loaded up and on their way back home, Myrtle was busy laying out the next edition of the *Charlotte's Town Beacon*. She had just finished printing the front page when she heard some commotion out in the street. She put down the page and went to look out her front door. Over in front of the sheriff's office, she saw Slocum and Judge Colter with Amos Dean in tow. Slocum and the judge dismounted and tied the three horses. Then Slocum hauled Amos out of the saddle. When Amos landed on the ground, he winced and limped. Townsend stepped out of his office just then. Myrtle grabbed up her new page and hurried across the street. Slocum was just shoving Amos through the door when she arrived.

"Put him in a cell," Judge Colter was saying.

"What's this all about?" said Townsend.

"Lock him up and we'll fill you in," said the judge.

Townsend picked up the keys from his desktop and took Amos by one arm to walk him over to the cell. "Come on, Amos," he said. Amos gave Townsend a look, and Townsend nodded to him, as if to say, "It will be all right." He ushered Amos into the cell and then shut and locked the door. He walked back to his desk and tossed down the keys. He turned and looked at Slocum and Colter. "Well?" he said. Myrtle stood in a corner of the room keeping her silence.

"This man and five others laid an ambush for us out on the road," said the judge. "The other five are dead. You'd better send someone out with a wagon. There are five horses out there too. All wearing the Tall T brand."

"It's all a lie, Mark," said Amos from inside his cell. "We was just out for a ride. That's all, and these two bastards commenced to shooting at us."

"That's his story," said the judge. "There will be a trial."

"Here's some evidence for you," said Myrtle, moving forward with her news page and holding it up for all to see. Judge Colter took it and held it up for a moment. Then he laid it out on the sheriff's desk. There under the banner was the drawing that Georgie McGuire had done, a child's rendition of an evil man holding a smoking gun, wearing a black shirt and hat, his features much like those of Amos Dean. Under the picture were these words. "Young Georgie McGuire's drawing of the man who murdered his parents, Charley and Ernestine McGuire, after trying in vain to make them sign some papers. Does this look like anyone you know?" Everyone turned to look at Amos.

"What?" Amos said. "What the hell is this all about? What?"

Colter picked up the page and walked toward the cell. He held it up for Amos to see. Amos's face went pale.

"You can't pin that on me," he said. "That's just a kid's drawing. It could be anyone. Besides, a kid like that what just seen his folks shot down, why, he's all messed up in the head. Has to be. That don't mean nothing."

"It sure is a good likeness of you," said Slocum.

"And he says that he can identify the killer," said Myrtle. "We may not have your boss, but we've got you dead to rights. The story of your hanging will be front-page news, and I can hardly wait."

Colter then expressed his ferocious desire for a good hot meal, and Myrtle invited him and Slocum to join her at the Ballard Hotel Restaurant for a meal. Colter said that he would pay for it, and they all walked over there. Before they left the sheriff's office, though, the judge admonished Townsend. "That man had better stay in jail," he said.

As soon as they were outside, Amos started yelling at Townsend. "You got to let me out of here," he said.

"I can't do that, Amos," said the sheriff. "Hell, it was the judge that put you in. Don't you know what that means? The judge. And you heard what he said when he walked out. You heard him. There's not a thing I can do."

"Well, you better think of something. I ain't swinging all by myself. I promise you that. If I go to trial and they say I'm going to hang, I'll start talking plenty. I'll talk you and Thornton right up there alongside of me. You go have a talk with Thornton, and the two of you better come up with some idea. I'm telling you."

"All right. All right. Just calm down. I'll do that. I'll have a talk with Thornton. Last I knew, he was right over there in his office."

Townsend put his hat on his head and started to leave the office. He had the door opened, but he stopped. "Here he comes right now," he said. He put his hat back on the peg in the wall and waited for Thornton to come in. Thornton brushed rudely past Townsend to look at Amos there in the cell.

"Get me out of here," said Amos.

"What the hell happened?" said Thornton.

"Slocum and Colter brought him in," said Townsend. "Said there was five more out there on the road dead."

Thornton stepped up to the cell door and glared through the bars at Amos. "What the hell happened?" he asked again.

"Well," said Amos, hanging his head, "we laid an ambush all right. Waited forever. I even sent Buber ahead to make sure they was coming. He seen them and come back and told us. Only somehow or other they knowed about it and snuck up behind us. Killed all the others, they did. I didn't have no chance, or else I wouldn't have give up."

"You've let Slocum get the drop on you twice now," said Thornton. "And that's after he knocked you down in the street in broad daylight."

"He caught me by surprise," said Amos.

"All three times?"

"Yeah. I'd a took him otherwise."

"Amos," said Thornton, "you're a lying skunk. The question now is what do we do about this situation."

"You can't let them take me to trial," said Amos. "That McGuire kid can identify me. He drawed my picture for the newspaper."

Thornton looked at Townsend, who nodded in agreement. "It was a pretty fair likeness too," he said. "Say, that kid can draw."

"That means you're likely to be charged with murder as

well as attempted murder," said Thornton to Amos.

"They'll hang me."

"That's likely," said Thornton.

"You can't let that happen."

"Mr. Thornton," said the sheriff, "Amos told me that he'll talk before he hangs. He'll tell them everything he knows—about you and about me—everything."

Thornton glared savagely at Amos. "Is that right?" he said.

"Well, I ain't going to hang all by myself," Amos said. "That's for sure."

"Shut up, Amos," said Thornton. "I'll get Lawyer Daggett for you. We'll get you out of this some way. Don't worry. You won't hang."

He turned and abruptly headed out the door, motioning Townsend to follow him. The sheriff put on his hat and went out the door behind Thornton, who had stopped on the sidewalk. The sun was low in the western sky already. "Come on," said Thornton. "Let's go have a drink."

They walked down the street to the saloon and went inside, finding a table not too close to where anyone else was sitting. Thornton made a gesture to the barkeep, who brought a bottle and two glasses and left them alone. Thornton poured two drinks. He took a long sip of his own. Townsend took a drink. Then Thornton leaned back in his chair. He wore a troubled look on his face.

"Townsend," he said, "there ain't no way to get Amos out of this mess, is there?"

"I sure can't see one," said the sheriff.

"He laid an ambush for Slocum and a goddamned federal judge at the same time. No one's word will stand up against that of Judge Colter."

"No one's," said Townsend, shaking his head sadly.

"On top of that, he went and killed a man and a woman and let their kids watch the whole thing and get away alive to be witnesses."

"Are kids that age fit to be witnesses in a legal court?" Townsend asked.

"Sure they are," said Thornton. "Don't you know nothing about the law? A jury's free to believe them or not, but with everything else they've got on Amos, the jury would believe the kids for sure."

"Amos said he'd talk."

"He won't go to trial."

"But you told him you'd get Lawyer Daggett."

"A white lie."

Thornton poured the glasses full again.

"How we going to keep him from being tried?" Townsend asked.

"Kill him," said Thornton.

In the restaurant at the Ballard Hotel, Slocum sat with Colter and Myrtle. They each had a drink, having just finished their meal. "There's only one thing, Your Honor," said Myrtle.

"What's that, my dear?" said Colter.

"We've got Amos dead to rights, but we still have no proof against Thornton. I know as well as anything that Thornton's behind it all, but how do we—"

"Tut-tut," Colter said. "Don't worry. I came down here prepared to investigate, and along the way we just got ourselves a little bonus. That's all. The investigation will go forth. Amos Dean will be tried and undoubtedly hanged. The investigation will still go forth."

"What are you planning to do?"

"Interview Mr. Thornton," said the judge.

"If he knows that you're onto him," said Slocum, "he might just panic and do something foolish."

"That's certainly a possibility," agreed the judge, "and I've thought about that. The other thing I can do is interview Mr. Amos Dean. He's a cowardly wretch. If he thinks there's a chance that spilling the beans on his boss will save his neck, he'll talk. I think he will."

"You'd let him go if he talked?" said Myrtle.

"I'd let him spend the rest of his life behind bars instead of hanging," said the judge. "That's my prerogative."

Myrtle sighed and leaned back in her chair. "I sure had

my mind set on watching him hang," she said. "Him and Thornton and the rest of their crew."

Colter ignored her. "The first thing in the morning," he said, "I'd like to talk to the little McGuire lad. Do you think you could ride along with me and show me the place?"

"Sure," said Myrtle. "I want to show them the newspaper anyway."

"Good. Then that's settled."

Slocum couldn't think of anything else, so he downed his whiskey, set the glass back on the table, and stood up. "I think I'll hit the sack," he said.

"An excellent idea," said Colter. "Do you have a place to stay?"

"I'm staying in the back room at the newspaper office," he said.

"Very well," said the judge. He held out his hand for Slocum to shake. "Slocum, we've had ourselves a hell of a day, haven't we?"

"We sure have," said Slocum. "Good night."

He walked out of the Ballard and across the street to the office of the *Beacon*. Myrtle had given him a key to the place since he was both working there and staying there, so he stopped to unlock the door. As he stepped inside and turned to lock the door behind him, he glanced through the window, and he could see Judge Colter and Myrtle standing on the sidewalk outside the Ballard, saying good night as he guessed. It was a good thing that they were old friends, he thought. They sure did need an old friend like the judge just now. He started to turn and make his way to the back room, but something made him stop and keep watching. Colter had a hand on Myrtle's shoulder. The scene looked awfully cozy. They stood there for a moment talking. Then Colter gestured toward the hotel door and Myrtle nodded. They turned and walked back into the hotel together.

"Why, that horny old bastard," Slocum muttered to himself. "That old son of a bitch."

11

The judge peeked into the hotel lobby, and no one was in sight except the night clerk. He was nodding in his chair. "Come along," the judge said, and he took Myrtle by the arm and led her quickly across the lobby and up the stairs. In the hallway, he unlocked the door to his room and stepped aside, allowing Myrtle to enter first. He stepped in behind her and closed and locked the door. He took off his hat and hung it on a peg, and as he turned, he turned right into her arms. She pulled him close to her and kissed him full on the lips, holding tight and long. Breaking the embrace at last, she started helping the judge out of his coat. "It's been much too long since I've seen you, my dear," said Colter.

"Way too long, Your Honor," said Myrtle. She put the judge's coat and vest on hooks and walked him to the bed, where he sat down on the edge. Myrtle knelt to pull off his boots.

"Ah," he said. "That's much better."

"It will get even better," she said.

She stood up and slipped the galluses off his shoulders. Then she helped him out of his shirt. He stood up to get his trousers off, and while he was doing that, Myrtle began stripping off her own clothes. Soon they were standing

97

naked, facing each other. They embraced tightly and kissed again, the judge becoming aroused at the feeling of her naked loveliness pressing against him, her firm breasts mashed against his chest, her bare arms wrapped around him, the wiry pubic hair tickling the tip of his cock, which was starting to rise already.

She broke the embrace and reached down to jerk the covers off the bed. Then she crawled in, and the judge watched her bare bottom as she did so. He liked the sight of what he saw. "I've had a long ride today," he said, "and I have a few more miles to go." He crawled in behind her, gripping her by the waist as he did, and she stayed on her hands and knees. "Lovely, lovely," he said.

"Mount up, Your Honor," she said.

"You've been found guilty, my dear," he said. "Now you must take your punishment."

"I'll take it," she said.

The judge aimed the head of his throbbing rod at her moist cunt, and she reached back with one hand to guide it in. "Ah, yes," he said. "Ah. Ah." And as he thrust forward, she backed up and took the full length of it into her all at once. She gasped at the feeling. "Oh, yes, Your Honor," she said. "Give it to me. Give it to me hard." And the judge began pounding away, causing her whole body to shake with his thrusts and causing the whole bed to rock and rattle.

At the Tall T Ranch, Thornton had called all his remaining gunnies into his office. There were sixteen of them altogether. They sat around the room lounging and drinking whiskey, which Thornton had graciously supplied. "Men," Thornton said, "I've called you all together tonight because there have been some developments that you need to know about. First of all, Amos is no longer in charge. He's in jail right now in Charlotte's Town."

"What for?" said a man hunkered up in an overstuffed chair against the wall.

"They've got him for murder and for attempted murder," said Thornton.

"Can't you handle that?" the man asked. "You got the sheriff in your pocket, ain't you?"

"One of the men Amos tried to kill was Judge Colter from the capital. Mark Townsend is backed against the wall and me along with him. We have to be real careful from here on."

"What if Amos starts to talking?"

"I've got that covered," said Thornton. "Don't worry about it. Starting right now, Beeler, you're in charge, but I don't want you doing nothing but acting like working cowhands. You got that? If you go into town, don't act up. Don't give no one any excuses to be locking you up or questioning you about nothing. Act like Sunday school teachers."

Slocum found sleep hard coming that night. He got up and stared out the window toward the jail. He didn't think that even Townsend would be fool enough to try anything that first night, but he couldn't be sure. Then he found his eyes wandering over to the hotel, wondering which of the rooms Judge Colter was in, wondering what the judge and Myrtle were up to in there. It was none of his business, though, and he pulled his eyes away and fastened them again on the jail. It was dark over there. There was no movement. No sign of life. Somewhere out in the lonesome night a dog barked.

Slocum was up early the next morning, and when he walked out onto the street, the judge and Myrtle were already out and mounted up. He found it difficult to look at them.

"Good morning, Slocum," said the judge.

Slocum tipped his hat.

"Good morning, Slocum," said Myrtle. "We're off to Morgan's place. I want to show them the paper, and Judge Colter wants to interview little Georgie."

"You want me to ride along?" Slocum asked.

"Won't be necessary," said the judge. "Better you stay here and keep your eyes on that jail. I don't trust that sheriff."

"All right," said Slocum, and the other two rode down the street headed out of town. Slocum watched them for a moment. Then he walked to the Ballard to get himself some breakfast. Going in, he almost ran into Jobe Thornton. He stepped aside.

"Slocum," said Thornton. "I'm glad to see you this morning."

"Oh?" said Slocum. "I can't figure why."

"I understand that my man Amos Dean tried to bushwhack you and the judge yesterday."

"You understand pretty good," said Slocum, "but he wasn't much successful."

"I know. He's over in the jail."

"Seems like a pretty good place for him. Best one I can think of except dangling from the end of a hanging rope."

"Uh, yes. I just wanted to let you know that whatever he did, I had no knowledge of it. Needless to say, he's no longer in my employ."

"Kind of hard to be employed sitting in a cell."

"Yes. Well, if he should ever get out, he won't be working for me."

"I doubt if he'll be getting out."

"I just wanted to have my say," Thornton said, and he tipped his hat and walked away.

Out at the Morgan place, Judge Colter and Myrtle sat at the table with the adults. The children were all sitting properly around the room. Tildy had poured four cups of coffee. The news page Myrtle had brought along was laid out on the table. "That had ought to cause some folks to stir," Randy said.

"Yes, it should," said the judge.

"Georgie," said Myrtle. "Did you see it?"

"No, ma'am."

"Well, come on over here and take a look."

Georgie stood up and walked to the table. He stared at the page intently with no comment.

"It's a good drawing, my boy," said the judge.

"It's ugly."

"Well, yes. It's a good drawing of an ugly, bad man, but we have that man in jail now. He's going to trial, and he's most likely going to hang for what he did."

Georgie's face lit up a little. Still, he said nothing.

"How does that make you feel, Georgie?" asked Myrtle. "Does it make you feel any better?"

"It won't bring Ma and Pa back," he said, "but I reckon it does help some little bit."

"Georgie," said the judge, "would you be willing to come to the trial and be questioned?"

"What about?"

"Someone will ask you to look at that man and tell them what you saw."

"Just to tell the truth about what happened and how you can recognize the man that did it," said Myrtle.

"Will that make him hang?" Georgie said.

"It will help," said the judge. "You're the only one who actually saw him do the deed. You and your little sister."

"Then I'll do it," Georgie said. "When they hang him, can I watch?"

There was silence all around for a moment. The adults all looked at one another. It was a grim thought to have a child of his age watching a hanging, but then, Colter thought, what he had already witnessed was grim enough, and they were asking him to play the part of a man. He thought it over quickly, and then he answered.

"Yes," he said. "You can be there."

Back in town, the sheriff brought a saddled horse into the alley behind the jail and left it just where Amos could see it looking out the cell window. He had decided that broad daylight would be the best time for his plan. No one would be expecting it. They would think that if anything were going to happen, it would be under cover of darkness. Besides, he knew that the judge and Myrtle had gone out of town, and all he had to worry about was Slocum. Slocum was not likely to be full on his guard. Townsend had been watching, and he knew that Slocum had gone into the newspaper office a few minutes ago. He had not come back out. Townsend was at his desk.

"What's Thornton up to?" Amos said from inside the cell.

"Don't worry," said Townsend. "We're working things out."

"How you working them out?"

"We're going to get you out of here. You won't have to stand trial at all."

"When? When you getting me out?"

"Right now," said Townsend, standing up from behind his desk. He picked up the keys and an unloaded .45 from off the top of his desk. He walked toward the cell. "Look out that window," he said. "There's a horse ready for you out there. See it?"

"I see it," said Amos.

Townsend unlocked the cell door and held the empty gun, butt first, out to Amos. Amos took it and examined it. He found it empty.

"What the hell is this?" he said. "What are you trying to pull on me?"

"We can't have any shots fired in town. It would bring the whole damn town down on us. There's bullets in the saddlebags. You can load up when you get out of town."

"How you going to explain this to the judge?"

"I'll just say that I don't have any idea where you got the gun, but you got the drop on me," said Townsend.

Amos looked down at Townsend's side and saw the loaded gun resting on his hip. He thought quickly. He considered that it would be prudent for Thornton just now to get rid of him. It would be easy as hell for Townsend to put a bullet in his back as he walked away.

"What am I supposed to do?" he said. "Just ride away from here? Leave the country? I'm stove up, and I'm broke."

"Thornton said for you to ride out by his ranch before you clear out, and he'll pay you off."

Amos paced across the room and looked out the front window toward Thornton's real-estate office, and he thought that he could see Thornton inside. Ride out to his ranch and he'll pay me off, huh? Amos thought. If I was to ride out there, I wouldn't find him to home.

"All right," he said, and he headed for the back door, but as he passed Townsend, he swung the empty revolver and struck Townsend a blow across the side of the head. Townsend's hands went up to his head as he groaned. "Ugh." He staggered back a couple of steps, and Amos followed, hitting him again on top of the head. Townsend crumpled to the floor. Amos leaned over and beat him again and again on the head until the empty gun was sticky with the sheriff's blood. "Liar," he said. "Lying son of a bitch."

He tossed the gun aside and bent over the body, going quickly through the pockets. He found forty dollars, which he pocketed, and he took the gun out of the dead sheriff's holster. Then he ran to the front window again and looked out onto the street. There were a few people milling around, but it looked clear enough to Amos. He hurried over to the gun cabinet on the wall and found a box of .45 shells, which he dropped into a pocket, and then he ran out the back door, mounted up, and headed out of town. No one saw him go.

Myrtle and the judge were riding along side by side on their way back to town. Myrtle said, "Little Georgie has sure been through a lot for a child his age. It shouldn't happen to any child."

"Yes," said the judge. "He's a good, strong boy, though, and he'll make a fine young man. I think I'm about ready to set the trial date now. I think I'll use Nathan Finch for the prosecutor. He's a good man. He'll work things the way I tell him to. Thornton will likely hire old Daggett to defend Amos Dean. It won't do him any good. The deck's stacked in our favor."

"What about Thornton?" said Myrtle.

"Oh, we'll get him. I still haven't talked with Amos Dean and made him an offer."

"Georgie will be awful disappointed if he doesn't hang."

"I know," said the judge. "I'll have to think on that. Maybe I'll have my talk with Thornton first. See if I can shake him up some."

They rode along for a while in silence. Then Myrtle said, "How long do you think you'll be in town, Your Honor?"

He looked over at her and smiled, and he said, "Oh, I'll be around long enough to put you on trial a few more times, my dear. A few more times."

Slocum tired of his studies in the newspaper office. He wasn't coming up with anything more than they already had. Not used to sitting around doing nothing when he knew there was a job to be done, he decided to get up and do something. He might be able to put the fright into Amos, he thought. He decided to walk over to the jail and give it a try. He left the newspaper office and strolled over to the jail. Opening the front door, he stepped inside. "Damn," he said. There was Mark Townsend lying on the floor in a widening pool of blood. The cell door was standing wide-open, and there was no sign of Amos. "Damn," he said again. He moved to Townsend and knelt down for a moment, but it did not take long to determine that the man was way the other side of needing help. His skull was bashed in horribly. The gun was missing from his holster. Slocum tried to figure what had happened. Either someone had slipped Amos a gun, or the sheriff had planned a fake jail break and it had backfired on him. Slocum noticed a bloody revolver on the floor a few feet away, and he went to examine it. It was empty. There would be plenty of time to try to figure out what had happened later. Right now, he thought, the important thing was that Amos was loose.

He hurried to the back door and looked out. At first he thought there was nothing to be seen. Then he noticed that a horse had been out there. The signs of fresh horse shit were clear enough. So Amos had some help. There was no doubt about that. He looked more closely, and he could tell that Amos had mounted the horse and lit out of town headed east. Slocum hurried down the street to the livery and got his Appaloosa. Then he took off following Amos's tracks. He meant to catch the son of a bitch, and this time, he meant to kill him.

12

Thornton was watching out the window of his real-estate office when he saw Slocum ride hard out of town. He wondered what had happened over at the jail. Townsend was supposed to have shot Amos while Amos was trying to escape. But Thornton had heard no shot, and now Slocum was racing out of town. Something must have gone wrong. He waited until Slocum was out of sight, and then he stepped out the door. He saw Elgin ambling along the sidewalk and hailed him over. "Did you see that Slocum riding moving out fast just now?" he asked Elgin.

"Yeah. Wonder what he was up to."

"I don't know. Let's you and me stroll over to the jailhouse and see if Mark knows anything."

"All right."

In another minute they were there, and they opened the door and stepped inside. They saw Townsend there lying dead.

"My God," said Elgin.

"So that's why he was moving out so fast," said Thornton. "He's murdered the sheriff."

"My God," said Elgin.

"Get over to the saloon. See if any of my boys is there. We'll form up a posse and get after the murdering bastard."

Elgin stood, mouth agape, staring at the body of Townsend and the spreading pool of blood.

"Go on, Elgin," said Thornton.

"Oh. Yeah. Okay."

Elgin turned and ran out of the office. Thornton looked at Townsend and smiled. He was thinking that he would be well rid of both Townsend and Amos. It was obvious that Amos had killed the sheriff. Mark Townsend had blundered the deal. It had backfired on him, and Amos had killed him instead of the other way around. Then Amos had run away. Slocum had stopped in and seen what had happened and was on Amos's trail. But that's not the way Thornton would spread the tale. He and Elgin had seen Slocum riding fast out of town. They had come running to investigate and had found poor Mark Townsend lying dead. Slocum was the killer. He turned and left the office. Already his men were gathering in front of the saloon, mounting their horses, ready to get on the trail of the killer.

Amos had gotten a couple of miles out of town before he had mercy on his horse and slowed it down. He had not had time to think before. Now he had to slow himself down and consider what he was going to do. He had killed the sheriff. Everyone in town would know it, including Slocum and that damned judge. Already they were planning to put him on trial for everything they could think of to charge him with. Now they would have no trouble convicting him and hanging him. That is, if they could catch him. He had a good head start, but he had only forty dollars in his jeans. That wouldn't last him long. He had a Colt .45 with six bullets in it, and a box of shells in his pocket. He wished he had grabbed a Winchester from the office, but he hadn't been thinking too clearly. He knew that he couldn't just ride out of the territory, though, with only forty bucks. He would have to get some money somewhere. He thought about riding out to Thornton's Tall T Ranch, but then he remembered that was just what Thornton and Townsend had wanted him to do. Besides, Thornton might not be there.

He might be in town at his office. He decided that Thornton likely was in town at his office, and he further decided that town was the last place anyone would be looking for Amos Dean. Well, he would fool them all. He would circle around and ride back into town. That's what he would do.

Slocum slowed his pace a little ways out of town. He could tell by the tracks that Amos was moving fast, but if he kept it up, he would ruin his horse. Slocum figured that he would catch up with the man sooner or later, but in a while, the tracks disappeared. The road had become rockier. Slocum continued riding until he came up on a rise. He could see well ahead on the road, but he saw no sign of Amos. He couldn't be that far away. He must have left the road somewhere back there behind. To his left the ground rose up to a ridge of rocky hills, partly covered with scrubby brush and pitiful little trees, all struggling to stay alive on the little rain that fell in this area. Slocum looked around for a way up. He spotted a place where his Appaloosa could make the climb without too much trouble, and he urged it in that direction. He was right. The climb was fairly easy, and he soon found himself up on top. He stood in his stirrups to gain as much height as possible, and he looked around in all directions. He saw no sign of Amos. There were several places, though, where a man could be riding and not be seen from up there. Then he saw the riders coming down the road. About twelve of them, he guessed. He figured further that they must be a posse from town on the trail of Amos. Someone else had gone into the sheriff's office and discovered the empty cell and Townsend's body on the floor. He decided to ride down to meet them. They could split up and cover more area quicker.

Back in Charlotte's Town, Thornton was still on the street. He had sent his riders out with Beeler in charge, and stayed behind to spread the word that a posse was out after Slocum, the man who had just murdered their sheriff.

Amazingly, the same people who had complained about Mark Townsend before suddenly forgot everything bad they had ever thought about the man. They were mourning his loss and hating the man they thought had killed him.

"I hope they bring him back alive," said one man, "so we can watch him hang."

Jobe Thornton was wearing a long face, but underneath it was a satisfied smirk. He was working himself out of a tight spot very nicely. It was beginning to look like everything would work out in his favor after all. He hoped that Slocum would find Amos and kill him before the posse caught up to Slocum, and once they caught him, he hoped they would kill him too. Then all of Thornton's problems would be solved. That's all it would take. He could handle the judge and the newspaperwoman all right.

Out on the road, one of the riders spotted Slocum coming down the hillside. He pointed and shouted, "There he is." Beeler pulled the rifle out of his saddle boot and cranked a shell into the chamber. "Cut him down," he ordered. All twelve men started shooting at once. Slocum fell out of the saddle, and the Appaloosa ran on down the hill and into the road. Slocum lay still on the hillside behind a large, low rock. Bullets were smacking into the dirt and rocks all around him. He had not had time to jerk his Winchester free, so he was trapped there with only his Colt, and there were twelve men or so down there firing at him. It had to be Thornton's bunch, he thought. It wasn't a legitimate posse after all. He had been a fool to think that it was. In another minute, the bullets had stopped. He lay still for a moment trying to hear the voices from the road. He could hear some shouting and distinguish different voices, but he could not make out anything they were saying. Then he heard the horses moving. They were coming closer. At last he heard the voices clearly.

"Marvin," someone said, "get down off your horse and go up there."

"What if he ain't dead?"

"Then kill the son of a bitch."

"I don't want to go up there," said Marvin. "He could be laying for us."

"I think we killed him," said the other one. "Hell, we musta shot five hundred bullets."

"I ain't going," said Marvin.

"Oh, hell, Beeler," said yet another one. "I'll go. I ain't scared like Marvin."

"I ain't scared, Pete," Marvin said. "Well, not exactly. I just ain't stupid."

"I ain't stupid either," said the one called Pete, "but someone's got to do it, and I'll go."

"All right," Beeler said. "Stop fussing about. Get on up there, Pete, and see if he's dead."

Pete gave a look of scorn to Marvin. Then he slowly swung down out of the saddle. He stood for a moment and hitched his britches. He checked his revolver to make sure it was sliding easily out of his holster, and then he started walking. He walked to the bottom of the hillside and started going up, as cautiously as he could manage, but he had to look down at the rising ground to take sure steps. He paused. He glanced back over his shoulder. "Someone come with me," he said.

"You're scared after all," said Marvin.

"Shut up," said Beeler. "Monkey, go with him."

Monkey got off his horse and started after Pete. Soon he was beside him. He looked at Pete questioningly. Pete said, "You watch the hillside in case he pops his head up. Watch while I walk. Then I'll stop and watch while you come up alongside of me."

"All right," Monkey said.

Pete moved on ahead a few more steps. He stopped and motioned Monkey to follow. Monkey caught up with him again. Pete moved ahead. They were within six feet of the rock that Slocum way lying behind. Suddenly Slocum showed himself, and his Colt barked. The slug tore into Pete's chest knocking him backward down the hill. Monkey screamed and turned and jumped, landing on his feet some distance down the hill, but falling forward when he did and landing on his face. He slid for a ways and then scrambled on his hands and knees. Pete lay still and dead. Slocum dropped back down. The men on horseback started shooting again, but they could not see what they were shooting at.

"Get down," cried Beeler. "Get off your horses and take cover."

The shooting slowed down as the men dismounted hurriedly and scurried for cover. Most of it was on the same side of the road as was Slocum. They crouched behind small clumps of brush or behind small boulders and looked up the hillside toward their prey. Marvin said, "He weren't scared, but he sure is dead."

"Shut up, Marvin," Beeler said. "Let's get him."

There were more shots fired up the hill. They stopped again. "Hell, Beeler," said Monkey, whose face was scratched up and bruised from his slide down the hill, "we can't see nothing."

"So what are we going to do?" said another.

"Shut up and let me think," said Beeler. It was quiet on the road and on the hillside. Beeler thought deeply for a spell, and then at last, he broke the eerie silence. "Slocum," he called out. "Hey, you, Slocum."

"I can hear you," Slocum answered.

"Slocum, if you give it up, we won't kill you. We'll take you into town and hold you for the judge."

"That sounds like bullshit to me," Slocum said. "Hold me for what?"

"For killing the sheriff."

"I didn't kill Townsend, and you know it," Slocum said. "I was on Amos Dean's trail when you came along."

"We don't know nothing about that," Beeler said. "All we know is that Thornton seen you riding hard outta town and went over to the sheriff's office and found him dead."

"And the cell empty and Amos gone," said Slocum. "I'll make you a deal. Mount up and head back to town, and I won't shoot."

"We can't do that. We was told to bring you in."

"I'll come in after you," Slocum said.

"I don't think we can trust you."

"The feeling is mutual," said Slocum, "so come on up and get me."

"Beeler," said Monkey in a harsh whisper, "we can't do that. Look what happened to Pete."

"I know what happened to Pete, goddammit," Beeler said. "We could all of us go up after him all at once. He couldn't get all of us."

"No, but which ones would he get? I don't want it to be me."

"Let's try again to smoke him out," Beeler said. "Everyone start in shooting."

Judge Colter and Myrtle were riding along side by side on their way back to Charlotte's Town from the Morgan place when they heard a barrage of shots from up ahead. They looked at one another. "What could that be?" Myrtle said.

"I don't know," said Colter, "but I mean to find out. You stay back behind me a ways. I don't want you getting hit."

He spurred his horse ahead, and Myrtle rode along behind him. Soon enough, the judge could see the men at the base of the hillside firing up into the rocks above them. He slowed his pace and moved ahead cautiously. The firing slowed down some, and Colter cried out in his loudest voice, "Hold your fire. This is Judge Colter. What the hell is going on here?"

Up ahead, Beeler said, "Hold your fire, boys. Trying to kill the judge is what got Amos in trouble."

Colter rode ahead. Slowly, one at a time, the men stood up to face him. He rode right up among them before he stopped his horse. "Put away those guns," he said. The men looked toward Beeler, and Beeler said, "Put them up, boys." They holstered their six-guns and lowered their rifles.

"Now," said Colter, "who are you shooting at up there?"

"It's Slocum," said Beeler. "He killed Mark Townsend. Thornton sent us after him."

Colter looked up the hillside. "Slocum," he called, "is that you up there?"

"It's me," Slocum answered.

"Come on down."

Slocum stood up slowly looking down at the men on the road. The judge was still sitting on his horse. Myrtle came riding up behind the judge. Slocum decided that it was safe enough, and he started walking down the steep hill.

"What's this about Mark Townsend?" Colter said. "Did you kill him?"

"No," Slocum said. "I never. I found the sheriff dead on his office floor and the cell door open. Amos Dean was gone. I rode out after Amos."

"You men mount up and head back for town," said Colter.

"What about Slocum?" Beeler said.

"Never you mind about Slocum," the judge snapped. "Just get."

Beeler and the others mounted up and started to move, but Judge Colter stopped them. Beeler looked back over his shoulder, and the judge nodded toward the body of Pete on the hillside. "Take that along with you," he said. Beeler designated two men to fetch the body, and soon they were all riding with dejected looks on their faces back toward Charlotte's Town. Slocum found his Appaloosa and mounted up.

"You came along in the nick of time," he said.

"It looks that way," said Colter. "So Amos escaped. He most likely killed Townsend, and you came along just in time for Thornton to try to pin it on you."

"That's what it looks like. I was on Amos's trail when that bunch of gunnies came along. Like a fool, I thought they were a posse after Amos, so I showed myself, and they just started shooting at me."

"With Amos gone, we're right back where we started," said Myrtle.

"Don't be so sure," said the judge. "We have some pretty damning circumstantial evidence against Thornton. I haven't even started yet. Come on, you two. Let's get into town."

Amos Dean rode into Charlotte's Town a back way. No one saw him. He rode down the alley to just behind Thornton's real-estate office. Looking both ways down the alley, he dismounted and tied his horse just by the back door. He tried the door and found it unlocked. He opened it and went inside. No one was there. He was afraid that Thornton might have gone out to his ranch, but he did not want to ride out there. He felt more or less secure there in the office. No one would be coming in there except Thornton. He decided to wait. He had no idea how long a wait he would have, but he made up his mind. He would wait if he had to wait all night. He needed to see Thornton. He meant to have some money from the man.

13

Thornton had quite a mob gathered on the main street of Charlotte's Town by the time his gang of outlaws came riding back into town with their long faces. The crowd was bellowing around as Thornton pulled Beeler off to one side. "Did you get him?" Thornton asked.

"We had pinned down, but the judge come riding up. Had that newspaperwoman with him. He made us quit and come back to town."

"Goddamn it," snarled Thornton.

"I didn't think you'd want me to kill the judge and the woman."

"You were right," said Thornton. "Forget it. Did you see any sign of Amos?"

"Never seen him at all. But Slocum killed Pete before the judge come along."

"All right. Never mind about that right now. Say. Here they come."

Beeler turned to see Slocum, Colter, and Myrtle riding into town. Someone in the mob saw them too and shouted out, "Here he comes. Let's get him." The mob started shouting even louder and rushing toward Slocum, but Judge Colter pulled out both of his Colts and fired them into the air. The mob stopped in its tracks, staring hard ahead.

"What do you people think you're doing?" the judge said.

"We mean to string up Slocum," someone said.

"He killed our sheriff," said another.

"That's right."

"Yeah."

Colter fired another round, and they shut up. "What makes you think Slocum did the killing?" said the judge. "You found the sheriff dead and the prisoner escaped. Doesn't it make sense that the escaped prisoner killed the sheriff? Did you ever think of that? Any blockhead should have thought of that. Slocum was riding after Amos Dean, and Thornton's bunch interfered with him, probably allowed Dean to get away. Slocum had to kill one of them defending himself. Now all of you damn fools go on back to your business and leave the law business to me. Go on now. Get."

Slowly, grumbling, the crowd broke up, men ambling off in different directions, some going home, some going back to work, others headed for the saloon. Inside Thornton's real-estate office, Amos Dean, having heard the commotion and the shots outside, went to the window to look out and see what was going on. He had seen the judge break up the mob and heard him tell them that Amos was the killer and not Slocum. He could see the judge, Myrtle, and Slocum still on their horses in the middle of the street, and he watched as they rode toward the sheriff's office. Then his heart skipped a beat as he saw Thornton walking toward the real-estate office with Beeler. So Beeler was the new ramrod, huh? He stepped back to stand behind the door when it opened. He waited, his stolen Colt in his hand.

As Slocum and the judge stepped into the sheriff's office, Colter held an arm out in front of Myrtle. "You don't need to see this," he said. She brushed past him.

"Yes, I do," she said. "I'm a newspaperwoman."

They all three moved on into the office.

"Nothing's changed," Slocum said. "It's just like I found it."

"And you never saw Amos Dean?" the judge asked.

"No, but I could see out back where someone had rode out fast on a horse. I followed after him."

"We'll charge Dean with the murder," said Colter, "along with all the other stuff we have on him already. If we can run him down, we'll have a trial that will set this town on edge."

"If we can run him down," said Myrtle.

At Thornton's real-estate office, Thornton opened the door and stepped inside. He was followed closely by Beeler, who stepped in and shut the door. Thornton walked over behind his desk and turned to sit down, and when he did, he saw Amos standing there beside the door with a gun in his hand. Thornton did not sit. He stood still. Beeler saw him and turned to see what he was staring at.

"Amos," he said.

"What are you doing in town?" said Thornton. "Don't you know that everyone is looking for you? They're saying that you killed Mark Townsend."

"Well, I did," said Amos. "He was trying to pull something on me."

"He was letting you out of jail," said Thornton.

"He give me an empty gun," said Amos. "I think he was fixing to kill me and say that he shot me while I was trying to escape."

"No," said Thornton. "That's crazy. Why would he do that?"

"Most likely on account of you told him to do it. They was fixing to put me on trial, and you was afraid I'd talk and tell them all about you. You couldn't have that, now could you?"

Beeler was looking nervously from Thornton to Amos, trying to figure out what to do.

"I told you that I was going to get you a lawyer," said Thornton. "But there was always a chance that they'd find you guilty anyway, so I told Mark to let you escape. I told him to tell you to ride out to my ranch, and I'd give you some money. I figured you'd need some money to help you along your way. Things had just got too hot for you around here. That's all. Now put that gun away, and I'll get you some money. You'll have to wait till dark, though, to slip out of town."

"I'll just hang onto this gun," said Amos, "but you can go on ahead and get me some cash."

"All right," Thornton said, "but don't shoot, for God's sake. You'll just bring the whole town down on us." He moved over to the big safe against the wall and knelt down to work the tumblers. He pulled open the door and reached in for a stack of bills. As he was turning to hand the money to Amos, Amos stopped him.

"You can give me more than that," he said. "Clean that safe out."

"You're robbing me?" said Thornton.

"Clean it out."

Beeler's eyes got big as he watched Thornton take several large stacks of cash out.

"You're taking all of my operating cash," said Thornton. "You're going to ruin me."

"That's real sad," Amos said. "Move away from that safe now."

Thornton stood up and backed toward his desk. Amos moved to the safe and ducked to look inside. Amos's gun was pointed carelessly at Thornton. Beeler saw his chance and pulled his own side arm out quickly, but Amos saw the movement out of the corner of his eye. He whirled to fire a shot at Beeler, but Beeler's shot rang out at almost the same time as Amos's. Amos nicked Beeler across the upper left arm. Beeler's shot tore through Amos's neck, causing his head to bob foolishly before he fell back, his head landing inside the safe. His eyes were wide-open, but they were unseeing. He was dead.

"Good work, Beeler," said Thornton.

"I'm hurt," said Beeler.

"Sit down. I'll get the doc."

Thornton ran to the front door and jerked it open. He yelled at the first man he saw on the street. "Get the doc," he said. "Beeler's been shot, and someone get the judge too. We got Amos Dean in here. Hurry it up."

Thornton was suddenly feeling much better. Amos Dean was no longer a threat. He turned back to Beeler inside the office.

"I guess it ain't too bad," Beeler said, "but it's throbbing some, and it's bleeding pretty bad."

"Doc'll be here in a minute," said Thornton. He hurriedly gathered up the money he had pulled from the safe. He looked at the safe, which was now chock-full of Amos's stupid-looking head, and he hurried on behind his desk to stuff the cash in a drawer. He would put it back in the safe after the judge had viewed Amos and had his remains removed. Dr. Brand came into the office carrying his black bag. He looked at Amos for a moment. "Over here, Doc," said Thornton, pointing toward Beeler. Doc moved over to tend to Beeler's wound. Just about then, Judge Colter, followed by Myrtle and Slocum, came into the office. He stopped and studied the scene in silence for a moment.

"Tell me about it, Thornton," he said.

"There's not much to tell, Judge," said Thornton. "Beeler and I just came in a few minutes ago. Amos was waiting with his gun in his hand. I told you, I think, Slocum, that he was no longer working for me."

"Yeah, you said that," Slocum agreed.

"Well, he made me open my safe. He meant to rob me. When his attention was diverted just a little bit, Beeler here got the best of him. That's all there is to tell. Oh yes, except, he did say that he had killed Mark Townsend. Slocum, I'm sorry about that earlier misunderstanding."

"Forget it," said Slocum.

"I'll need a signed statement of all that," the judge said.

"Sure," said Thornton. "I'll take care of it."

Colter turned to face Beeler. "You going to be all right?" he asked.

"Yeah," said Beeler. "Sure. I'll make it."

"There's nothing more to do here," said Colter, "except for the undertaker. Let's go."

Colter, Slocum, and Myrtle were walking back toward the sheriff's office. "I've got a mess of paperwork to take care of now," Colter said, "but we need to have someone ride back out to Morgan's place and bring little Georgie in to take a look at Amos before they plant him."

"Is that necessary?" asked Myrtle.

"It is," said Colter. "It may be more necessary for Georgie than for any other reason."

"I'll ride back out," Myrtle said.

"I don't know—"

"I'll go with her," said Slocum.

"All right. But keep an eagle eye out. Be careful."

"I don't think there's any immediate danger, Judge," said Slocum, "but I'll watch out for it just the same."

"You do that."

Colter went on back into the sheriff's office, and Myrtle and Slocum mounted their horses again and headed back toward Morgan's place.

Colter had the sheriff's body removed, and had a woman come in and mop the floor. He sat at Townsend's desk and reloaded his six-guns. At last he settled down to work. He took out the papers that Slocum had shown him initially back in his own office, and using them as a guide, he made his own list. He wrote down the names of all the people whose property had been acquired by Thornton and what had happened to those people, whether they had disappeared or been murdered. Then he bracketed the names and wrote in the margin, "Amos Dean was in the employ of Jobe Thornton at this time." He got a fresh piece of paper and listed all the charges against Amos, beginning with Amos's attack on poor Sammy Sneed and noting that

Sammy had been shot and killed just a little later by "persons unknown." He listed Amos as the accused murderer of the McGuires, and made a note regarding the drawing that little Georgie McGuire had done. He listed Amos's attempted killing of Slocum and later of Slocum and himself. Then he wrote a report of the escape from jail and the killing of Sheriff Mark Townsend. He also noted the theory that Townsend had been in the employ of Thornton all along, and that he had been planning to kill Amos during a phony escape for Thornton. He made mention of the fact that Thornton had tried to convince the town that Slocum had killed the sheriff. His final notes described the report of Thornton and Beeler regarding the demise of Amos Dean.

He leaned back and heaved a sigh, looking at his notes. It was true that all evidence against Thornton was circumstantial. A good lawyer would be able to pull Thornton out of the trouble that he was in, unless a jury could be convinced of the man's guilt. That was always a possibility, but Colter did not really want to go to trial with just that hope. He wanted to be more sure of himself, more confident in the outcome. It was late and he wanted a drink. He left the sheriff's office, and was headed for the saloon when Myrtle and Slocum came back in the company of Randal Morgan and Georgie McGuire. He met them in the middle of the street and walked along beside them to the undertaker's parlor. There they all went inside. The judge had the body of Amos Dean uncovered for Georgie to look at.

"That's him," Georgie said. "That's the man that killed my pappa and mama."

"Are you sure about that?" Colter asked him.

"Of course he's sure," said Myrtle.

"I'll never forget him," Georgie said. "He's the one."

"All right," said the judge. "That's all we need. Thank you very much, young man. We'll take it from here."

They walked back outside. Morgan and Georgie headed back for their horses. "If you two want to spend the night in town," said Colter, "my office will pay for the room."

"Thanks just the same, Your Honor," said Morgan, "but I don't want to leave Tildy and the rest of the kids out there all alone overnight."

"It's a pretty long ride. You'll be late in getting there," said the judge.

"I'll ride along with them," said Slocum.

"You don't have to do that," said Morgan.

"If you don't mind," said Slocum, "I'd like to."

As Slocum rode out of town again in the company of Randal and Georgie, Myrtle and Colter stood a moment watching them go. Then the judge said, "I was just on my way to the saloon for a drink when you all came riding in."

"Is the newspaper office just as good?" Myrtle asked. "I have a good bottle of bourbon over there."

"It'll do nicely," said the judge.

Harlan Snippet sat uncomfortably in the stagecoach that bounced and rocked along the road. He had one more day before arriving at his destination of Charlotte's Town. Damn, but the coach was a dreadfully wretched way to travel. The fat woman sitting next to him was suddenly jounced over against him, and he winced. "Pardon me," she said.

"It's quite all right," he replied.

The coach hit a bump in the road and almost leapt into the air, tossing all the passengers up off their seats. They landed back again with thumps and moans. Snippet was certainly going to be glad when this journey was over. He had not wanted the job, but it had been handed to him anyway, along with comments that strongly implied he could either take it or leave it, and leave it meant his job. He could not afford to lose his job, so he had taken it, but he did not have to like it. He did not like anything about this rough Western country. He was much more at home in Boston.

He had not minded it too much when they had sent him to Kansas City, but this was almost too much. This ghastly frontier. Oh, well, when he arrived at Charlotte's Town, he would check the local land office against his maps, locate all the necessary rights-of-way, and then set about the business of acquiring them for the railroad. It shouldn't be too difficult a job, and he figured that he could wrap it all up in a matter of a few days. Once that was done, he would have to endure the horrible stagecoach ride once again. At the end of it, he would be able to transfer to a railroad again—finally. He was looking forward to that. Then the railroad would be moving into this part of the world, and no one would ever again be forced to submit to such a ride, at least not to this particular part of the country.

Beeler went into the big ranch house to see Thornton. He found his boss sitting behind his desk looking at papers with a glass of whiskey on the desk in front of him.

"I got to talk to you, Boss," he said.

"Pour yourself a drink," said Thornton.

Beeler poured one and took a chair across the desk from Thornton.

"A bunch of the boys is talking about quitting," he said. "They're saying that things is getting to be too hot around here. They think that the judge is after you, and they don't want to get caught up in that."

"What do you think?"

Beeler thought about all that money he had seen in Thornton's office in town. "I'm sticking with you, but I ain't been able to convince the boys."

"Let them go," said Thornton. "To hell with them. You and me will clean up here in just a few more days."

14

Thornton did not want to be facing all of his problems alone, so he was glad to have Beeler stick with him. He was not worried about losing the others, though. They really did not matter much to him. It had been nice to have a full crew earlier, when he had needed it, but he no longer felt the need. He did not really think that he would have any trouble with the judge. When the evidence was presented that Amos had killed the McGuires and that the little boy was a witness, all Thornton had to do was to claim that he had not known what Amos was doing. He had not ordered it done, and Amos had acted on his own. And in spite of what everyone thought about Thornton wanting to control the whole valley, he really did not need it. He had most of the rights-of-way the railroad would be wanting to buy, and that included a good deal of his own ranch. He had already sold all of his cattle. He would sell the land to the railroad, pocket the money, and clear out. He thought that he could figure out a way to get rid of Beeler along the way too. Then he would have all the money to himself. He could go anywhere. Kansas City. New Orleans. Maybe San Francisco. He would be a wealthy son of a bitch, and he could settle down to a respectable life. The buyer from the railroad was due in town just any day now. Thornton was getting anxious.

First thing in the morning, he gave Beeler enough money to pay off the deserting cowards. He did not even go out to face them and say good-bye. He didn't give a shit about them anyway. Beeler took the money out to the bunkhouse, where the men were all just about ready to ride. He paid each man five dollars less than what Thornton what given him to pay them, and no one questioned the amount. They felt pretty good that they were getting out while the getting was good. Besides, they hadn't done much lately to earn their keep anyhow. They pocketed the cash and climbed into their saddles.

"Beeler," said Monkey. "You sure you won't come along with us? I got a bad feeling about this place. It's fixing to crash in on ole Thornton."

"I told him I'd stick, and I ain't going back on my word."

"Well, if you change your mind," Monkey said, "you'll find us down in New Mexico. I hear tell there's a range war a-brewing down there."

"I'll keep it in mind," said Beeler, "but don't be watching for me."

The boys rode out, and Beeler watched them go. Then he walked back to the ranch house. Thornton had just stepped out on the porch.

"They all leave?" he asked.

"Every last one of them," Beeler said.

"All the more for you and me," said Thornton. "It won't be long now."

Judge Colter had added to his notes that Georgie McGuire had positively identified the body of Amos Dean as the man who had murdered his parents, and Colter had added to the note the information that Amos had definitely still been working for Thornton at the time. Even so, he knew that all he had was enough circumstantial evidence to merit an investigation. He knew that Slocum and Myrtle were frustrated. Probably a bunch of others were too. There had to be some way of getting at Thornton, but he just couldn't hit on any solid plan. He had finished his breakfast and a couple of extra cups of coffee. He was on his way back to the sheriff's office, which had by this time become his own temporary office, when he saw Thornton and Beeler riding into town. He waved them down. "I want to talk to you in the office," he said.

"Which office?" asked Thornton.

"The sheriff's office," said Colter. "Right now."

The two men rode to the front of the sheriff's office, dismounted, and tied their horses to the hitch rail there. By then Colter had arrived. He walked in first, and they followed. Colter moved behind the sheriff's desk and sat down. He motioned to a couple of chairs, and the other two sat opposite him.

"What can we do for you, Judge?" Thornton asked.

"I have some questions I need to ask you, Thornton," said Colter. "I should tell you first that I have been asked to conduct an official investigation into the going-on around here. Private citizens have been beaten and murdered, and you seem to have been the main beneficiary of all these shenanigans."

"Now just a minute, Judge—"

"Hold on. I haven't asked a question yet. I have a list here of all the people who have either been killed or have mysteriously disappeared, and their land holdings have been acquired by you." He read through the list. "Is that an accurate listing?"

"Yes, it is," said Thornton. "I hired Amos Dean to act as my agent and purchase those particular tracts. That was all I told him to do. I had no idea that he using strong-arm tactics, as you have accused. If he did that, he was acting on his own initiative, and not on my orders. When it became clear that he was behaving like a ruffian, I fired him."

"Now, am I correct in assuming that you were buying up land in preparation for the arrival of a railroad purchasing agent? And that you were keeping that information a secret?"

"Why, yes," Thornton said. "That may be a little sneaky, but there's nothing illegal about it, is there?"

"No. No, there isn't. Were you aware that on the very day that Miss Myrtle Gilligan published an article unflattering to you, Amos Dean beat her employee Sammy Sneed in broad daylight and attempted to take all the papers the man was selling, and would have done so if it had not been for the interference of the man called Slocum, and that just a short time later, on that same day, Sneed was shot from ambush and killed?"

"I heard of it after the fact. I had no knowledge of any of it beforehand."

"You were displeased at the things that Miss Gilligan was publishing about you, were you not?"

"Of course I was. Who wouldn't have been. They were libelous."

"And you did not set Amos Dean upon her man?"

"Of course not. That would have been against the law. I was considering hiring a lawyer to sue her for libel."

"Why didn't you?"

"She stopped writing those things. I decided to let well enough alone."

"You weren't afraid that a lawsuit would bring too many things out in public?"

"What kinds of things?"

"The railroad coming to town, for instance."

"It couldn't have done that. She didn't know about it at that time."

"Your land purchases and the dead or vanished men?"

"No. I had not yet made that connection myself. I was unaware of what Amos had been doing."

In the newspaper office, Myrtle was busy writing up all the latest news: the story of the capture of Amos Dean and of his escape and the murder of the sheriff, the expected arrival of the railroad purchasing agent, the killing of Amos Dean, the identification of Amos Dean as the murderer of the McGuires, the presence of Judge Colter in Charlotte's Town, and his ongoing investigation of the many crimes in the valley in recent months. She was excited as she had not been in a long time. She was doing her best writing. She was careful not to make any accusations that she could not back up, but if the implications pointed fingers at Jobe Thornton, so be it. She was so engrossed in her job that she was startled when the door opened and Slocum came walking in.

"Oh," she said. "I was busy. You surprised me."

"What you writing?" he asked.

"The latest news. Nothing that can get me in trouble."

"That's good," he said. He walked over to look over her shoulder and see what she was writing.

"Did you get Randal and Georgie home all right?" she asked.

"No problems," he said. "I don't think they're in any danger anymore. All Georgie could do was identify Amos as the man who killed his folks. He did that, and Amos is dead anyhow."

"I guess you're right," she said.

"Say, I could use some breakfast. Can you take a break from that?"

She put down her pencil and straightened up. "I guess I could," she said. "Let's go."

When they walked out of the office, they saw Thornton and Beeler coming out of the sheriff's office and walking toward Thornton's real-estate office. They paused and looked at one another.

"I wonder what that's all about," Myrtle said.

"Let's go find out," said Slocum, and they angled toward the sheriff's office.

"I don't like it, Boss," Beeler was saying.

"Shut up," said Thornton. He led the way into his office and shut the door behind them. "Now," he said. "You were saying?"

"I said I don't like it. The judge is for sure after you. He suspicions you of giving orders for all them killings that Amos done, and he means to bring you down."

"He doesn't have anything on me," Thornton said. "If he did, I'd be in jail right now."

"But he's investigating. He said it."

"Let him investigate. He won't find anything. What can he find?"

"I still don't like it."

"If you don't like it, then get out like all the others did. It will be just that much more money for me. Look, as soon as that railroad man gets to town, I'll make the sales. Then you and me will clear out of here for good."

"All right," said Beeler, thinking again of all the money he had seen. "I sure hope he hurries along, though."

Slocum and Myrtle talked the judge into joining them for breakfast. They had finished their meal and were drinking another cup of coffee. "I've got him nervous," Colter was saying. "That's about all for now. I don't have a bit of evidence on him. Only on Amos Dean. And by the way, he's let all his employees go except for Beeler."

"What do you make of that?" Slocum asked.

"He's through with his strong-man tactics," said Colter. "He's ready to sell out as soon as the railroad agent hits town, and then he's getting out with the money."

"We can't let that happen," said Myrtle.

"Right now," said Colter, "I don't see any way to avoid it."

In the hill country west of town, Monkey and the rest of the former employees of Jobe Thornton had stopped for a rest. They had built a small fire and boiled up some coffee. A few of them were making small talk, but Monkey sat pondering something, staring back toward Charlotte's Town. Finally he broke his silence, standing up and addressing the whole crowd.

"Boys," he said, "I got something to say." They all shut up and turned toward him attentive. He went on. "There's something up back yonder that we walked out on. We might have got out too soon."

"What are you talking about?" one asked.

"Well, it did seem like the time to get out. I'll admit that. I was one of the first to say it. What with that gunslinger Slocum and then that hellfire judge come to town, it was looking bad."

"We all agreed with that."

"Not all. Beeler stayed behind."

"If he's that stupid, that's his business."

"That's just it," Monkey continued. "Beeler ain't stupid. And he ain't in love with Thornton neither. No. He knows something that the rest of us don't know."

"Like what?"

"I ain't sure of that. That's just the trouble. If I was sure, I'd know what to do."

"You ain't thinking about riding back in there, are you?"

"No. Not just yet."

"Well, what then?"

"I ain't sure. That's how come I'm talking it over with you."

One shooter, who had been sitting to the back of the bunch and had not spoken up as yet, said, "If Beeler's staying behind, there's got to be money in it."

"That's what I'm thinking," said Monkey. "Lots of money."

It was around noon in Charlotte's Town when the stagecoach lurched to a stop in front of the depot. Harlan Snippet was the first to step out. The driver and shotgun were tossing down pieces of luggage, and as soon as his hit the ground, Snippet grabbed it up and headed for the nearest hotel. He got a room, washed his face, gathered up his papers, and left again. He soon found the land office and went inside. It wasn't long before he was on his way to the Thornton real-estate office. He reached the office and opened the door, stepping inside. Thornton was sitting behind his desk. He looked up.

"What can I do for you?" he said.

"My name is Harlan Snippet. I represent the railroad."

"Oh, yes," said Thornton. He jumped up with a big smile on his face and extended a hand. "I've been expecting you. Sit down. Sit down. Oh, yes, this is my associate, Mr. Beeler."

Beeler shook hands with Snippet. "How do," Beeler said.

"Shall we get right down to business?" Snippet said. "I don't want to stay in this town any longer than I have to."

"We feel exactly the same way, Mr. Snippet," said Thornton.

Snippet laid out his papers on the desk. "These are the tracts of land I'm interested in," he said. "I understand that you own most of them."

Thornton glanced briefly at the papers. "Yes," he said. "I do."

Snippet took out a small piece of paper and wrote on it. He shoved the paper across the desk toward Thornton. "This is my offer," he said. Beeler sneaked a look, and his eyes opened wide. Thornton looked at the paper, crossed out the figure Snippet had written, and wrote another. He shoved the paper back across the desk.

"This is my price," he said.

Snippet looked and raised his eyebrows. "You're asking way too much, Mr. Thornton," he said. "My offer is firm."

"Look, Snippet," said Thornton, "You and I both know that the railroad needs that land. There's no other way for it go. You have to get that land, and I have it. You have to meet my price."

Snippet wrote another figure on the paper and shoved it back. Thornton looked at it and shook his head. "No," he said. "I've given you my price."

Snippet gathered his papers back up and shoved them into his bag. He stood up in a huff. "You're making my stay in this town very difficult," he said. He turned and headed for the door.

"You'll be back," said Thornton. Snippet walked out and slammed the door.

"Boss," said Beeler, "what the hell's the matter with you? He made a hell of a good offer. I ain't never seen that much money."

"He'll pay more," Thornton said. "He's going to the telegraph office and send his bosses a wire. They'll authorize him to spend more money. He'll be back with it tomorrow. Wait and see."

He was half right. Snippet went straight to the telegraph office. Inside, he sent a wire that said in part, "Thornton is the main seller. He wants way too much. Won't deal. Advise."

He paid for the wire and then looked at the telegrapher. "You will let me know when I get a response?" he said.

"I'll run it right over to the Ballard, sir," the man said.

15

"You know your boss is about due for a hard fall, don't you?" Slocum asked Beeler one evening, standing at the bar in the saloon. Several days had passed since the arrival of Harlan Snippet, and everyone was on edge. Nothing was happening. Judge Colter continued to harass Thornton regularly, and Thornton was growing more and more irritable. He had threatened the judge with legal action, but he knew that it was an idle threat. Colter was the highest legal authority in the territory. The newspaper had carried no stories of real interest since Myrtle's stories right after the killing of Amos Dean. Snippet had received a response to his wire. It had only said, "Sit tight. Help is on the way." He hated every minute he had to spend in Charlotte's Town, and had begun to wish that a tornado would come through and take the place right off the map. Of course, he had not considered where he would be when this disaster finally came about. Out in the hills, Monkey and the other hard cases were restless and anxious for action. A couple of fights had broken out among them. Their camp was growing filthier every day. They were low on supplies. And every now and then, when Slocum ran into Beeler in town, he did his best to torment Beeler and break him down.

"I don't know what you're talking about," Beeler responded to Slocum's question. "Why don't you just leave me be."

"I'm trying to help you, Beeler," Slocum said. "You still have time to get out of this clean."

"Out of what?"

"The whole mess that Thornton has got himself into. He'll be charged with murder and conspiracy at least. If he don't hang, he'll die in prison. If you stick around, you'll get the same—or worse."

"I don't believe you, Slocum. If the judge had anything on Thornton, he'd have him in jail right now. You're just trying to run a bluff on me. That's all."

"Suppose you're right," Slocum said. "Suppose the judge never does get Thornton in a courtroom. What do you reckon that'll mean?"

"Well, nothing. Just nothing."

"The people in this town know what's been going on, and they're getting fed up waiting on the judge. Just look around you. See how everyone is glaring at you? If Colter don't get you—or Thornton—in court, the town's going to rise up over it. Have you ever seen an angry mob go after someone? It can get pretty ugly, I tell you. I seen a mob one time rip a man's ear off before they finally strung him up. He was thankful when the end came."

Beeler tossed down the remains of his drink. "Shut up," he said, and he turned on his heel and hurried out of the saloon. Slocum motioned to the bartender for another whiskey.

Snippet was in his room at the Ballard with his shoes and his shirt off, lying back on the bed sweating and hating his circumstances, when a knock came at the door. He jumped to a sitting position, nervous anticipation on his face. "Who is it?" he called.

"Sidney Wilder," came the response.

Snippet bolted up from the bed. "Just a minute, Mr. Wilder," he said. "I'm not dressed."

"Open the goddamn door or I'll break it in," said Wilder.

"Yes. Yes," said Snippet, hurrying to the door, unlocking it, and jerking it open. He stared in awe at a small man, about five feet seven inches tall, with a drooping black mustache and black hair flowing down onto his shoulders, a man with cold blue eyes, wearing a black three-piece suit. In his left hand, he held loosely a Marlin rifle, and there were two Remington revolvers hanging from a belt around his waist. He also wore two shoulder holsters in which were snugged two British Webley "Bulldog" pistols. Nervously, Snippet held out his hand, but Wilder just brushed past him and stepped into the room.

"Shut the door," he said.

"Yes, sir," said Snippet, and he closed the door and turned to face Wilder.

"Mr. Howard sent me," Wilder said.

"Yes. I have his wire."

Wilder shot Snippet an angry look. "Did it mention my name?" he said.

"Oh, no. No. It just said, 'Help is on the way.' That's all. I didn't know who would be coming, but I've heard of you, of course. They say you're the best."

"Who's the problem," said Wilder, "and where do I find him?"

"His name is Jobe Thornton. He holds title to all—well, almost all—of the land in question. He has a ranch just east of town called the Tall T. But he's let all his hands go except one, and he's sold all his cattle. He seems to have been spending all or most of his time right here in town lately. He has a real-estate office right over there."

Snippet hurried to the window and pointed, but Wilder made no move. "Who's the hand he kept on?" he asked.

"A man called Beeler," Snippet said.

"Never heard of him," Wilder said. "Get dressed."

Snippet hurriedly started pulling on his shirt. "May I ask where are we going?" he said.

"When did you last make your offer to Thornton?" Wilder asked.

"Well," said Snippet, tucking in his shirttail, "it was the

day I sent the wire. He turned me down flat and asked for twice what I had offered him."

"You're going back in that office and make the same offer again."

"He'll just laugh at me," said Snippet.

"He won't laugh," said Wilder. "I promise you."

Snippet stepped into Thornton's office and found him there behind his desk. Beeler was there too, lounging in a chair against the wall. Thornton looked up as Snippet stepped in. He smiled.

"I knew you'd be back, Snippet," he said. "Did you get a positive answer to your wire?"

"I had my answer several days ago, Mr. Thornton," Snippet said.

"And what was it?"

"The offer remains the same."

"My answer is the same," Thornton said, the smile having disappeared from his face.

"The answer to my wire said that help was coming," Snippet said.

Thornton looked at Snippet and then over to Beeler and back at Snippet again. "What does that mean? What kind of help?"

Snippet stepped over to the window and pulled the curtain aside. He glanced out and smiled. He looked back at Thornton. "They sent a colleague to work with me. He's never failed."

Thornton hurried over to the window and looked out. He was followed closely by Beeler, who peered over his shoulder. Standing across the street, leaning casually against the front wall of the Ballard Hotel, was Sidney Wilder, all five of his weapons displayed prominently. Thornton nodded toward him. "That?" he said.

"My colleague," said Snippet.

"Who the hell is that?" Beeler said.

Thornton recovered his composure quickly, and said,

"It doesn't matter who he is. I'm not selling unless you meet my price."

"But, Boss—"

"Shut up, Beeler. This is my play."

"Is that your final word, Mr. Thornton?"

"That's it," said Thornton. "Don't come back unless you're ready to cough up the bucks."

"Very well," said Snippet, still smiling. "Good day to you." He tipped his derby hat, turned, and walked out of the office. On the sidewalk he paused. Across the street a man in a dark suit was talking to Wilder. He decided to wait.

Judge Colter had spotted the dangerous-looking stranger lounging against the Ballard's front wall. He had stopped and said, "Howdy, stranger." Wilder had only nodded.

"What brings you to Charlotte's Town?"

"Business."

"What is your business?"

"Who's asking?"

"I'm Territorial Judge Ira Colter. I'm in town on a special investigation. What's your name?"

Wilder heaved a sigh. "Sidney Wilder. I work for the railroad."

"You're working with Mr. Snippet?"

"That's right."

The judge looked Wilder up and down. Wilder was still holding the Henry in his left hand. His coat was pulled back to reveal all four revolvers. "You don't have the look of a railroad man," Colter said.

"I don't know what a railroad man is supposed to look like," Wilder said, "but you do look like a judge. Of course, I knew a man once who looked very much like you. He was a bank robber."

"I take your meaning, Mr. Wilder. I suppose I'll be seeing you around."

"I won't be in town very long," Wilder said.

When the judge had moved on, Snippet came scurrying across the street. "That was Judge Colter," he said.

"We met."

"What did he want?"

"Just wanted to get acquainted. What happened across the street?"

"He's still holding out," Snippet said. "I pointed you out to him, but it didn't seem to bother him. I do think that the sight of you shook up his associate, Mr. Beeler, but Thornton stayed firm."

Wilder started walking across the street toward the real-estate office. Snippet started after him, hesitated, and said, "Where are you going?"

"To meet Mr. Thornton," said Wilder.

"Do you want me along?"

"No."

Wilder walked to the office door and opened it. He stood there on the sidewalk for a moment looking into the office. He could see Thornton sitting behind his desk. Thornton could see him too. He sat and stared, his mouth hanging open. Wilder stepped inside, and then he saw Beeler sitting in his chair. Beeler got up to his feet. Wilder could see fear in Beeler's face, but in Thornton's all he saw was a kind of astonishment. Wilder moved across the room to stand directly in front of Thornton, and he laid his Henry rifle on Thornton's desk. Thornton pulled himself together. He stood up and extended his hand. Wilder ignored it.

"I'm Jobe Thornton. What can I do for you?"

"I'm Sidney Wilder. I work for the railroad."

"With Mr. Snippet?"

"He also works for the railroad."

"I see."

"I understand you've refused the offer Mr. Snippet made to you."

"I did. It's much too low."

"It's a fair price, Thornton. Take it."

"I've given Mr. Snippet my answer," Thornton said.

"I won't be back to discuss this further with you," said Wilder, "but I think you should know that the railroad gets what it wants."

Without another word, Wilder picked up his rifle, turned, and walked out the door. Thornton and Beeler were silent for a moment afterward. At last Beeler moved over to Thornton's desk. "Boss?" he said.

"What?"

"That man's a killer. That's the man the railroad sends out to get the land that folks won't sell to them, or that folks wants too much money for. Take Snippet's offer."

"I'm not taking a penny less than what I want," said Thornton.

"Like the man said, it's a fair price. It's more money than I ever thought to see in my whole life. And it's damn sure better than a bullet in your back."

"It's a bluff, Beeler," said Thornton. "You saw the way the man was posing across the street, the way Snippet pointed him out to us. And whenever did you ever see a real gunfighter all loaded down like that with weapons? He's a showman. He's doing his job, and it's working with you. He's got you running scared. The railroad does not send out murderers to acquire land. They've got more money than the pope. They'll meet my price when they see that they can't scare me."

"Yeah? Well how long will that take? And how far will ole Colter's investigation go by that time? You said I'm scared. Well, I am. I want out of here."

"You do? You want out? Well, go on. Get out then. Cut yourself out of all that money. It just means the more for me."

"So long, Thornton," said Beeler, and he turned and walked out of the office.

"Slocum," said Judge Colter, "do you know a man named Sidney Wilder?"

"I never met him, but I've heard of him," Slocum said. "He's a dangerous killer, if you're on the wrong side of him. The last I heard he was working for the railroad as a kind of troubleshooter, if you know what I mean."

They were sitting in the newspaper office. Myrtle was busy at the composing table. Colter and Slocum each had a cup of coffee, and Slocum was smoking a cigar.

"Meaning that when land acquisitions get troublesome, they send Wilder in," said the judge.

"That's about it."

"He's in town. I met him out on the street. He's wearing four revolvers and carrying a Henry rifle. He told me that he worked for the railroad, but I couldn't get any more than that out of him."

"Thornton must be trying to gouge Snippet," said Slocum, "and so they sent in Wilder."

"That's about what I figured," said the judge.

Myrtle shoved aside the work she had been doing to clear a space on the table. She grabbed a clean sheet of paper and a pencil and started writing.

> Notorious gunman Sidney Wilder, who works for the railroad in land acquisitions, is in Charlotte's Town, armed to the teeth. Speculation is that Jobe Thornton, who acquired the bulk of the land the railroad wants for its right-of-way, is being stubborn and that Wilder has been sent in to deal with him. How? We can't say. It's an interesting situation in that Thornton acquired the land himself under mysterious and suspicious means. The whole town, in fact the entire valley population, will wait and watch anxiously for further developments.

When she had finished, she read it out loud to Slocum and the judge. Then she looked at them in anticipation. "Well?" she said.

"Well what?" said Slocum.

"Well, shall I run it?"

"On the front page," said Colter. "Stick it right in their faces."

16

Beeler was riding away from Charlotte's Town with mixed feelings. He was glad to be getting away from Thornton and his problems, but he was also thinking about all the money that Thornton had in his safe, or in his desk drawer, wherever he had it by this time, and of all the money that could be coming from the railroad. Once or twice he almost decided to turn around and go back, but he kept going instead. He had no idea where he was going. He was just getting away. He thought about what Monkey had said to him about the rest of the bunch riding into New Mexico to hunt up a potential range war. That meant that nothing was happening there yet, but there were ways of spurring one on to get it going. But he really did not want to try to catch up with them either. They were a pretty nasty bunch, untrustworthy and unreliable, unless someone was paying them enough money to keep them more or less in line. He had about decided to cross the hills ahead and see what kind of a place he would blunder into. He had started riding into the foothills when a shot rang out. He reined in his horse and strained his eyes looking for whoever it might be shooting.

"Hold it right where you're at," came a voice. "Who are you and where're you headed?"

"My name's Beeler," he answered. "I'm just drifting."

"Beeler? Well, goddamn."

Beeler looked confused. As he looked around, a rider came out from behind some boulder on the hillside above him, slapping leather. When the man came closer, Beeler recognized one of the former Thornton gunnies called Pauley. The man made it down to where Beeler still sat calmly in the saddle.

"Beeler, what the hell are you doing out here?"

"Howdy, Pauley. Like I said, I'm just drifting. I quit that goddamned Thornton."

"Well, son of a bitch."

"What are you doing out here all by your lonesome?"

"Oh, hell, I was just watching to see who might come riding along. Monkey and the rest of them are on up yonder a ways."

"I thought you all'd be well on your way down to New Mexico by this time."

"Well, Monkey kinda decided that we'd hang around a spell. He figgered that you knowed something that we don't know, and that was how come you to stay behind like you done. I guess he was wrong, though, on accounta you having quit ole Thornton."

"Well, he wasn't exactly wrong," said Beeler. "There's big money involved all right, but it got to looking a bit too chancy for just the two of us, and that's how come I quit."

"Well, come along with me, and let's go see the boys," said Pauley. He turned his horse and led the way on up the hillside.

Back in Charlotte's Town, Thornton was sitting at his desk. He had already taken all his money out of the bank. He was ready to leave town as soon as Snippet came around to paying him off, and he was convinced that Snippet would pay. He did not believe that the railroad hired professional killers to get the land for them. He did believe that Wilder was there just to throw a scare into him. Besides, what good would it do the railroad to have the owner of land killed? He would no longer be around to sign over the deeds. Snippet would come around, and he would come around soon. Thornton was packed and ready to go.

But just at that same time, a small tin filled with black gunpowder and fitted with a fuse was sitting by the back door of Thornton Realty in the alley. The fuse was lit and burning down. There was no one in sight in the alley. The fuse burned slowly, scattering its sparks. Finally the sparkling disappeared down inside the tin, and then there was a loud explosion, and the alley was filled with dust and debris and smoke and the acrid smell of gunpowder. Thornton's back door fell into the office, and smoke and debris followed it. Thornton jumped up from his seat, pulled out his six-gun, and looked around for someone, but all he could see was the invading cloud of dust and smoke. He waved his arm in front of him and coughed and hacked. He ran out the front door. People were already gathering in the street in front of his office, and now that the front door was open, the cloud of smoke and dust drifted out through the opening into the street.

"What hell was that?" someone said.

"Someone just tried to blow my office up," said Thornton said.

"Did you see him?"

"Hell, no."

Colter and Slocum came trotting up.

"Are you hurt?" Colter said.

"No," said Thornton.

That's too bad, Slocum thought, but he kept the thought to himself. He followed the judge into the office. Holding their arms over their noses, they walked through the building, into the alley. Looking up and down, they saw no one. There were no footprints plain enough to be read. Slocum studied the blown-down back door and the ground below it in the alley.

"What do you think?" asked the judge.

"It wasn't a very big explosion," Slocum said.

"You mean—"

"Whoever done it wasn't trying to do ole Thornton any real harm. Just trying to throw a scare into him. That's all."

"You mean, like posing Wilder across the street from Thornton's office?"

Slocum shrugged. He walked back through the dusky office followed by the judge. When they reappeared back out on the street, Thornton rushed up to them. "Well?" he said.

"There's no real damage done," said Colter. "You'll need a new door."

"To hell with it," said Thornton. "I'll let it lay. I won't be around here much longer anyhow."

"You can say that again," said Slocum.

"What do you mean by that?" Thornton snapped.

"Oh, nothing."

"To hell with you too," said Thornton. He looked back at his office. Smoke was still drifting through. Leaving the front door standing open, he strode toward the saloon. People asked him questions as he walked by, but he ignored them. He barged into the saloon and stopped at the bar, where he ordered a large whiskey. He lifted the glass and took a long drink. As he lowered the glass, in the mirror, he saw Sidney Wilder sitting at a table back behind him. Wilder was smiling.

"Hey, Monkey," Pauley shouted as he rode into the outlaw camp, "look what I found."

Monkey looked up to see Beeler riding alongside Pauley. Both men dismounted, and the gang gathered around Beeler to slap his back and shake his hand. Monkey kept his distance and studied Beeler with curiosity.

"He's quit ole Thornton," said Pauley.

"Is that right?" Monkey asked.

"That's right," said Beeler.

"Want some coffee, Beeler?" said Pauley.

"Yeah. Thanks."

Pauley went to pour a cup from the pot over the fire.

"How come?" said Monkey.

"How come what?"

"How come you quit Thornton?"

Pauley returned and handed Beeler a steaming cup of hot java. Beeler took a tentative sip. "Thanks, Pauley." He looked around, and found a rock about the right size and sat down on it. Monkey squatted on his haunches looking Beeler in the eyes.

"How come you quit?" he said.

"Maybe I ought to tell you first how come I stayed on when the rest of you left."

"That'll do," Monkey said.

"I don't know if you fellas had any idea about the railroad coming through the valley."

"We'd heard some talk, but there didn't seem to be nothing happening."

"That's why Thornton was grabbing up all that land. It's land the railroad wants for right-of-way."

"That makes sense," said Monkey.

"Well, I knew about that," said Beeler. "And I seen all the cash that Thornton had whenever he give me the money to pay you all off. Then Amos come slipping back in town, and he showed up in Thornton's office and tried to rob him, and I seen a bunch more of money."

"How much?" said Monkey.

"Oh, hell, I don't know. Stacks of bills. Stacks and stacks."

"Well, shit and damn."

"Then a railroad man came into town to start in buying up land. Eastern dude. Name of Snippet. He come to see Thornton and made him an offer. A damn good one, but Thornton turned him down flat and wanted twice as much. Well, I could see what Thornton was up to then, and I argued with him about turning down all that money, but he said that the railroad would come across, and for me to just be patient."

"That sneaky son of a bitch," said Monkey.

"Yeah, well, the railroad man did send a wire off, and we waited some days, but when the answer to his wire showed up, it was a man named Sidney Wilder."

"I know Wilder," said a man back in the crowd. "He's a mean son of a bitch."

"Well, he works for the railroad," said Beeler. "I never seen such a man before. He ain't too big, but he was wearing four six-guns and toting a Henry rifle."

"Damn."

"He come over to the office, and he says to Thornton, 'The railroad gets what it's after.' That's what he said. Well, I took his meaning, but Thornton never. I argued with him, but he wouldn't budge. That's when I quit and rode out. Slocum and that two-gun judge was bad enough, but now that Wilder feller is in town too, and they're all lined up against Thornton. It was just too much for me. Well, that's it."

Everyone sat quiet for a time. Monkey stood up and walked around stroking his chin. Beeler sipped his coffee. Suddenly Monkey whirled around to face Beeler again.

"They might have been too much for you, Beeler, but there's ten of us here—eleven now that you're back. If the bunch of us can't handle them four men, then we ain't worth much, are we?"

"Handle them how, Monkey?"

"If nothing else comes to us, we can just ride into town and take the son of a bitch over. It's been done before. Eleven men can do it. We'll kill Slocum and the judge and Thornton, and then—"

"Hold on," Beeler said. "We can't kill Thornton. Not till he's signed over them deeds."

"Well, all right. Better yet, let him sell the land to the railroad man, and then kill him and all the rest and just take the money and ride out. How's that?"

"It might work. It sure is a lot of money."

"Are you with us then?"

"Who's in charge?"

"Well," Monkey said after he strolled up and down a few paces, "you was in charge when we quit, and you seem to know more about this setup than any of the rest of us. You can be in charge, and me, I'm second in command."

Visions of the stacks of bills he had seen in Thornton's office and of the note with the amount of the railroad's offer on it swarmed through Beeler's mind.

"It sounds all right to me," he said.

"All right," said Monkey, a wide grin on his face as he shook hands vigorously with Beeler, "let's get going then."

"Wait a minute," said Beeler. "Who'd you say was in charge?"

"Why, you are."

"Then I'll say when we get going. Right now we'll set here a spell longer and draw up some plans."

"All right. All right. Whatever you say."

"Is there anyone here with us who ain't been seen by either Slocum or the judge?" Beeler asked.

"They ain't never saw me," said a young runt toward the back. He stood up and moved forward. It was Jimmy Schlitz. Because of the sound of his name, the others had dubbed him Shitty Jim, and he had always put up with it, sometimes seeming to be proud of the name.

"Okay," said Beeler, "here's what I want you to do. Ride back to town. Keep yourself out of trouble. Just lay low and keep your eyes and ears open. We need to know if Thornton ever makes that deal with the railroad, and anything else important that might happen. We'll all move our camp back closer into town, and when we get to the right spot, we'll stop there, and you'll ride on. We'll wait there to hear from you."

Thornton was really pissed off. He knew that Wilder had blown his back door off in an attempt to scare him into signing the papers with the railroad. He also knew that if he held out long enough, the railroad would meet his price, and he was determined to hang on. The only problem was just what and how much was he supposed to put up with in the meantime. He could not count on any help from the law either. Mark Townsend was dead, and Judge Colter was the law in the territory. Colter was after him already. It would do no good to complain to the judge. He had already seen that. It would be dark soon, and he had to decide what to do with himself. He did not want to stay in town. Wilder might pull something else on him. He decided to ride back out to his ranch and sleep the night there. He already had all his money in a carpetbag, which he kept with him all the time. He did not need anything else. There was whiskey at the ranch. That was all he would need. He went to the livery stable and rented a horse and saddle from Sam Black. He tied the carpetbag to the saddle horn and mounted up. As he rode out of town, he saw Sidney Wilder standing on the sidewalk watching him. He spurred the horse viciously and hurried on past.

A short distance out of town, he slowed the horse down and rode along at a more leisurely pace. A strange thought occurred to him. What if it had not been Wilder who had blown his back door in? What if Slocum had done it, or even Judge Colter? He wouldn't put it past any of them. Even that goddamned newspaper gal, Gilligan. As he traveled the road to his ranch alone, he realized just how many enemies he had made in these parts. He thought about how glad and how relieved he would be to get his business all wrapped up and to get the hell as far away from Charlotte's Town as he could get. He thought about the bumbling gunmen he had hired. Amos, who never did anything right. And Beeler and the rest of the cowards who had all run out him when the going got a little tough. Well, good riddance to them all. He would think about them now and then when he was safe and secure in San Francisco—or wherever he decided to light. He would think about them riding the dusty range, punching cows, or shooting and getting shot at, and he would have a good laugh.

He rounded a curve in the road. It was now but a short distance on to his ranch. He thought about how the ranch would be a lonely place with no one around. He would be out there in his big house all along. He wondered if he had made a mistake, if he should have gotten himself a room in the Ballard Hotel for the night, but then he recalled that Snippet was there and so was Wilder. Judge Colter too. He did not want to be sleeping near any of them, much less near all of them. He spurred the horse ahead, anxious to settle into the seeming security of his home. But it wouldn't be his home for long. When the railroad finally paid him off, he would leave it behind, it and everything and everybody in this whole damn godforsaken place, this hellhole of the West.

A shot rang out, and the bullet tore the hat off his head. He yelled out in fright and fell from the horse rolling into the ditch beside the road. The horse, still carrying his carpetbag containing all his cash, ran off down the road. The sun was low in the western sky. It would be dark soon. He lay there in the ditch trembling with fear. The shot had been way too close for a shot only intended to frighten him. And his money was gone.

17

Shitty Jim wandered into Charlotte's Town and put up his horse at the stable. He ambled down the street until he came to a hotel, not the Ballard, but a much shabbier place. He got himself a room, put his roll in it, and wandered back downstairs. He strolled over to the Ballard and went inside for a meal. He looked around at what appeared to be opulence after the place he had roosted in, and he smirked. Finished with his meal, he walked back outside. Standing on the sidewalk, he rolled a cigarette, a twisted, wretched-looking thing, and lit it. He went on down the street till he came to the saloon, and he went inside. Bellied up to the bar, he ordered a beer. He tried to listen to all the conversations that were taking place, but when he managed to hear anything, it was unimportant. Outside again, he walked past Thornton's real-estate office, and he could see the front door standing open. He looked in and saw the back door on the floor. The place still smelled of burnt gunpowder. Someone came walking down the sidewalk, and Shitty Jim stopped him.

"Say, what happened here?" he asked.

"Someone blowed Thornton's back door in," the man said. "No one was hurt. Speculation is that it was the railroad men trying to scare him on account of he won't sell to them. At least, not at their price."

Shitty Jim thought about going inside to have a look around, but he decided against the idea. Thornton would not have left anything of value in there. Not with the place wide-open. And what if someone saw him nosing around? It wouldn't look good, and Beeler had told him to keep his nose clean. He walked on. As he did, he saw a man step out of the front door of the Ballard. He had never seen the man before, but he recognized him immediately from the descriptions he had heard. It was Sidney Wilder. A cold chill ran up Shitty Jim's back. He thought that Wilder looked like the devil himself. As Wilder moved on down the street, Shitty Jim shook off the feeling of dread and decided to be bold. He crossed the street and went into the sheriff's office. He knew that the man behind the desk was Judge Colter, knew that Sheriff Townsend was dead, but he played ignorant.

"Howdy," he said, and he smiled big.

Colter looked up. "Hello, friend. What can I do for you."

"You the sheriff?"

"No, I'm not. The town is right now without a sheriff. I'm Territorial Judge Ira Colter."

"I see," said Shitty Jim. "Well, my name is Jimmy Schlitz, and I was in town looking for some real estate to maybe purchase. I went over by that place—what was it called?"

"Thornton's?" said Colter.

"Yeah. That was it. Wasn't nobody there, and it looked kind of a mess. Someone told me that it was bombed. Is that right?"

"A person unknown blew the back door off its hinges," said Colter.

"Well, where's Mr. Thornton, the owner?"

"I'm afraid I don't know. He was in town yesterday. Have you checked in the saloon?"

"Yes, sir."

"You might check the Ballard to see if he's gotten a room there. If not, I would guess that he might have gone out to his ranch last night. He'll most likely be back in to his office sometime today."

"Well, all right. Thank you, sir," said Shitty Jim, and he walked back out on the street. He stood there for a moment thinking. He had learned something already, and it was interesting, but he did not think that it was enough for him to ride out to the camp to report to the others. He would just hang around town a little longer.

Thornton had lain in the ditch for what had seemed to him like hours. It was well after dark when he finally got up the nerve to stand up and walk down the road to his ranch house. It was pitch dark. It was deserted. There was not a cow or a horse on the place. He knew that it would be like that for he had sold everything off, and he had fired all his crew, except for Beeler, who had quit on him. His feet were hurting and his muscles ached from all the walking. He was not used to walking. He staggered up onto the porch and into the house. He thought about lighting a lamp, but instead he just fumbled his way in the dark into the bedroom and fell across the bed. In spite of all his worries, he was asleep almost immediately. That had all been the night before.

He woke up late, and his first thought was of his lost money. The money was the most important, of course, but the loss of the horse was also an immediate concern, since he was out on the ranch afoot. He got up out of the bed, and the pain and misery of the night before all returned to him at once. He had not undressed the night before, had not even pulled off his boots. He walked outside to the pump and dampened his head. Then he straightened himself up and looked around. There was no sign of a horse. He had hoped that the goddamned thing had wandered onto his ranch, but of course it had not. Well, there was nothing else for it but to go out onto the road.

He managed the walk back out to the road, and then he stood there and looked toward town. He saw nothing, no one. He looked the other direction, the way the horse had run. The road was empty that way as well. He hated to think of walking farther away from town than he already was, but the horse and the money were both in that direction. If he found them, everything would be all right, but if he failed to find them, he would be that much worse off. There was a curve in the road ahead, and he imagined that the horse would be right around that curve contentedly grazing alongside the road. He walked in that direction.

Myrtle Gilligan was glad about the explosion at Thornton's office. She was glad that something had happened to rile Thornton and to throw a scare into him, and she was glad that it gave her another story. She sat at her table in the newspaper office and wrote with glee. She had sold out of her previous edition, largely because of the story about Sidney Wilder. This one would sell out as well, she felt certain. Slocum was in the office too, but he decided to leave Myrtle alone with her writing. He thought that he'd stroll over to the sheriff's office and have a talk with the judge, but once he got outside, he spotted Wilder sitting in a chair on the sidewalk in front of the Ballard. He wasn't sure why, but he walked toward Wilder. Soon Wilder noticed his approach. He stood up to wait. When Slocum drew near, Wilder said, "You'd be Slocum. I've heard of you."

Slocum stopped walking and looked at Wilder. "And you'd be Wilder. I've heard of you too."

"Let me buy you a drink, Slocum."

Without another word, the two men crossed the street and went into the saloon. Wilder waved at the bartender and walked to a table back against the wall. Slocum followed along. In a moment, the barkeep brought a bottle and two glasses and left them on the table. Wilder poured two drinks and shoved one toward Slocum. They lifted their glasses and took a sip. Then they put their glasses back down.

"I've been wondering, Slocum," said Wilder. "What's your stake in this game?"

"I'm working for the newspaper lady," Slocum said.

Wilder laughed. "There's more than that," he said. "Come on."

"All right," Slocum said. "When I hit town, there were some murders taking place. The property of each murdered man wound up in Jobe Thornton's hands. No one could prove anything, though. So we got together what information we had, and I went for Judge Colter. He came back here with me to conduct an investigation. We figured out that Thornton was trying to grab up all the land that was in the way of the railroad right-of-way. Still couldn't prove anything, though."

"When did you go into the Good Samaritan business, Slocum?"

Slocum took another drink. He sat thoughtful for a moment, and he tried to recall just what Sammy Sneed had looked like. "Thornton's man Amos Dean killed a fellow right here in town," he said. "A harmless fellow. It was my fault."

"So we're both after the same son of a bitch," said Wilder, "but you're after justice, and all I want is to do my job and make sure the railroad gets the land it needs."

Slocum gave Wilder a sly look. "Did you blow Thornton's back door off?" he asked.

Wilder grinned. "You'd have a hard time proving that," he said. "Did you do it?"

"So what's your next move?" Slocum asked, ignoring the question.

"Wait him out," said Wilder. "Just wait him out."

Thornton had rounded two curves in the road and was limping badly. He knew that there was a small ranch up ahead not far, and he had decided to stop there and beg for a ride to town. But when he rounded the curve, he saw the horse. He saw the horse, but there was a man there with it. The man had gotten off his own horse and was about to open the carpetbag. In spite of his miserable feet, Thornton raced ahead, pulling out his revolver as he ran.

"Hey. You," he shouted. "Put down that bag. That's mine."

The man stopped what he was doing and dropped the carpetbag to the ground.

"I was just looking to see if there was any identification in there," the man said. "I come on this horse standing in the road. No one around."

"Yeah. Well, it's my horse. Did you open that bag?"

"No, I just—"

Thornton fired a shot, and the man fell dead. Both horses bolted and ran. One ran right past Thornton. He tried to stop it, but it got away. The other ran in the opposite direction. Thornton cursed, but he ran ahead to retrieve the carpetbag, which the man had dropped to the ground. He picked it up and snatched it open. The money all appeared to be still in place. He glanced at the body of the unfortunate man.

"I don't believe you," he said, as if the man could hear him. "You were trying to steal my money."

Holding onto the bag firmly, Thornton started walking toward town. He was lucky. The horse that had run past him was the one he had rented, and it hadn't run far. It took him a little while, but he managed to catch up to it and climb into the saddle. As he rode toward town, he thought that his luck had changed. Surely, when he arrived back in town, Snippet would be ready to deal with him. The railroad could not wait forever.

Shitty Jim walked into the saloon and saw Slocum sitting with Wilder. He tried to remain disinterested, and he ordered a drink at the bar. He was thinking that now he had two bits of news for Beeler and the others. Here were Slocum and Wilder getting chummy. He strained to hear the conversation, but their voices were much too low, and they were sitting too far away. He finished his drink and left the bar. He was standing on the sidewalk rolling another cigarette when he saw Thornton come riding into town. He was not wearing a hat. His clothes were rumpled and his hair was mussed. He rode straight to the sheriff's office and dismounted, quickly lapping the reins of his horse around the rail. Then, clutching a carpetbag in his arms, he hurried inside the office. Shitty Jim wondered just what the hell was going on.

"Judge," Thornton cried out as he entered the office. "Someone tried to kill me last night."

Colter looked up. "Who was it?" he asked.

"How would I know?" said Thornton. "He shot at me from ambush. Knocked the hat right off my head. I fell into the ditch and lay there half the night afraid that he might try again."

"You do look pretty rugged," said Colter. "Why don't you go over to the Ballard and get yourself a room. Have a bath. You'll feel better after that."

"I don't want a bath. I want you to do something."

"There's not much I can do if you don't know who it was that took a shot at you," said the judge.

"Damn it," said Thornton. "First someone tried to blow me up in my office, and then someone takes a shot at me. A man is entitled to protection by the law."

"I could take a ride out there and look around," said Colter, "but I doubt if I'd find any evidence."

"Oh, hell, Judge, you and I both know who did it. It was that damned Wilder, the railroad man. He's after me because I won't sell out to the railroad, not at their price."

"So what would happen to the deeds to your land if you were to be killed, and how would the railroad get their hands on it?"

"Well, I—I don't know. Oh, maybe it was Slocum."

"Why would Slocum want to kill you?"

"He's had it in for me ever since he hit town. That newspaper gal turned him against me."

"As far as that goes, Thornton, I've got it in for you too. I believe that you're the man behind all the unsolved killings around here. And the disappearances. I believe that you are guilty of murder, whether you did it yourself or hired it done. And I intend to see that you pay for it. So you see, with your reasoning, I might have blown down your back door, and I might have shot the hat off your head. By the way, what are you carrying in that bag that's so important? You sure are clutching it tight."

"Nothing," said Thornton. "I mean, it's none of your business."

He turned and rushed out of the office. In another minute, Slocum walked in. He didn't know it, but Shitty Jim had followed him and was lurking outside the window.

"I just saw Thornton go rushing out of here," Slocum said. "He looks a mess."

Colter smiled at Slocum. "He spent the night sleeping in a ditch," he said. "Someone took a shot at him. Knocked his hat off. He's scared to death. He thinks that you did it."

"I wouldn't have just knocked his hat off," Slocum said.

The judge laughed. "He come in here wanting me to arrest everyone in town. Wilder. You. Then I told him that it could have been me that took a shot at him, and that's when he went running out of here mad."

"Myrtle will want to hear about this," Slocum said. "It'll give her another story to write about."

The judge chuckled.

Outside, Shitty Jim turned casually and started strolling toward the stable. He thought that now he had something to tell to Beeler and Monkey and the rest. There were things happening all right, and the way they were going, things could break loose just any minute. He did not think that they could afford to wait much longer. They would have to ride in and take over the town. They would . . . He paused and watched Thornton hurry into the Ballard Hotel. He changed directions and followed Thornton. He got into the lobby just in time to see Thornton disappearing up the stairs. He followed. As he stepped onto the landing and looked down the hallway, he saw Thornton knocking on a door. He held back not wanting to be spotted. The door opened and Thornton went into the room. Shitty Jim hurried down the hallway to lurk outside the door.

"I'll take it," he heard Thornton's voice say from inside the room. "I'll take your offer."

Another voice responded. "I'm glad to hear that, Mr. Thornton. We'll have to go over to the bank to conclude our transaction."

"Will I get my money today?"

"Of course. As soon as the paperwork is all in order."

Shitty Jim hurried away from the door and then strolled casually back downstairs and out to the street. He walked a little faster on his way to the stable. He paid Sam Black, saddled his horse, and rode out of town as fast as he could go.

18

Wilder stepped into the sheriff's office with a smile on his face. He tipped his hat to Slocum and to Colter. "Gentlemen," he said.

"To what do we owe this visit?" said Colter.

"I just stopped by to tell you that we've won. Thornton's accepted our offer. He's over in the bank right now with Snippet. I came to say good-bye to you. I'll be leaving town first thing in the morning."

He turned and left the office. The judge grabbed a piece of paper and a pen. He dipped the pen in ink and wrote hastily. In another minute, he stood up, taking the paper, and hurried out the door.

"Judge, what—"

The judge was gone before Slocum could finish his question. He grabbed his hat and followed him. On the way to the bank, he stopped briefly at the newspaper office, just long enough to open the door and call out, "Something's up at the bank, Myrtle." Then he hurried on his way. Myrtle jumped up from her work and followed.

Inside the bank, Colter found Thornton sitting in front of a desk with Snippet seated beside him. Across the desk the bank president was writing. Colter strode to the desk and slapped his paper on top of it in front of them all.

"This is a legal paper," he said, "stopping all proceedings on this matter. Thornton's land ownership is under investigation."

The banker looked up puzzled. Thornton sprang up from his chair. "You can't do this," he shouted.

"I can and I have," said Colter.

Snippet sighed and put away his papers. He stood up. "I'll be in the hotel, gentlemen," he said, "if anyone wants me for anything."

Thornton moved close to Colter. Desperation showed on his face. "Judge, you've got to let this deal go through. Look. I'm leaving town as soon as it's done. Someone's been trying to kill me. You know that."

"A number of people have been killed, Thornton," said the judge. "Besides, I don't think you're in any real danger. Not of being murdered at any rate."

Colter turned his back on Thornton and walked toward the door. "Damn you," Thornton shouted. "Damn you to hell."

The banker stood up behind his desk. "Mr. Thornton," he said in a stern voice, "we can't have this kind of behavior in the bank."

Thornton looked at the banker. "Oh, fuck you," he said, and stormed out. He went to the saloon and bought a bottle of whiskey. Then he went to his office. Inside, he moved his chair into a back corner. Then he moved the desk over in front of it. He went behind the desk, took out his revolver, and put it on the desk, then sat down and poured a drink. He stayed there all the next day and night. During that same period, Snippet stayed in his room at the hotel, appearing out in public only long enough to take his meals. Colter was working furiously trying to build a case against Thornton. Myrtle was busy writing and publishing the paper with the new stories. Someone came into town with the body of the owner of a small ranch. He had found the body in the road. There was no evidence of any kind about who might have done the killing. Slocum was just hanging around.

The morning of the following day, Beeler's gang came riding into town. They rode fast, shooting their guns at anybody in the street. Their primary target was the sheriff's office, where they knew that Slocum and the judge spent much of their time. Clustered in the street in front of the office, they fired into the office, through the windows, through the door, through the walls.

"Cut them to pieces," Beeler shouted.

Charlotte's Town had been invaded, and it sounded like a war. Inside the office, Judge Colter was alone. When the shooting started, he turned the desk over and crouched behind it, drawing out both his Colts. He did not have a clear target, though. He just huddled there waiting it out.

Slocum was in the back room of the newspaper office. When he heard the shots, he grabbed his Winchester and ran for the front door. Looking out, he saw the outlaw gang. He cranked a shell into the chamber of his rifle and took aim. He fired, and one outlaw dropped from his saddle. A couple of others noticed the shot and turned to fire back at Slocum. He ducked back inside the office. Glass shattered around him from the front windows.

"Keep it up, boys," said Beeler as he turned his own horse to ride toward the real-estate office. At the front door, he dismounted quickly and ran inside. He stopped abruptly when he saw Thornton's gun pointed at him and the frightened face of Thornton behind it. But Thornton did not fire.

"Beeler?" he said.

"Yeah, Boss," said Beeler. "It's me. I come back. I got to thinking that you might need some help here."

"I need help, Beeler. You've got to get me out of here."

"Come on then," said Beeler. "I've got you covered. I've got horses out here. Come on."

Thornton came slowly out from behind his desk. He was still holding his revolver and clutching the carpetbag. The fighting outside was still raging. As Thornton moved toward the front door, Beeler stepped aside. Thornton paused in the doorway. There was but one horse there, and just down the street a battle was raging. "Go on," said Beeler. "Mount up and head out of town. I'll grab another horse and be right behind you."

Thornton turned to look outside once more, and Beeler fired, sending a shot into his back. Thornton twitched. He turned to look at Beeler with unbelieving eyes. He tried to raise his weapon, but his hand wouldn't respond. His fingers relaxed, and he dropped the gun. Still clutching the carpetbag, he fell back against the door, and then he slowly lid down to the floor, where he stayed in a sitting position, the bag in his lap, his unseeing eyes staring straight ahead. Beeler grabbed the bag and opened it. He did not think that the railroad money was in there, because if Thornton had gotten it, he would not be in town. Still, there was more money in the bag than Beeler had ever seen. He looked out at the fight going on in the street. He looked at the money. He ran out to his horse and jumped in the saddle. Turning the horse, he headed it out of town as fast as he could make it go, carrying the carpetbag in his left hand.

From an upstairs window in the Ballard Hotel, Wilder watched as Beeler rode out of town. He drew one of his Remingtons and aimed, but he did not shoot. The rider was too far away, and he knew that he would never hit the target. He holstered the Remington and went across the room for his Henry rifle. Back at the window, he no longer saw Beeler. The wretch had escaped him. He turned toward the melee in the street and took aim. His shot knocked a man from the saddle. Monkey hollered, "Dismount and take cover." The outlaws ran for doorways, for the corners of buildings. Shitty Jim ducked behind a watering trough.

Inside the sheriff's office, Judge Colter had crawled out from behind the desk to the front door, which had been hit by so many bullets that it had swung open. The judge peered around the corner looking for a target. Across the street, Shitty Jim raised his head above the trough to look for a shot. The judge hit him smack between the eyes.

Myrtle was on the floor in the newspaper office behind a desk writing as fast as she could write. Dodging bullets out in the street, Monkey stepped into the office. He did not see Myrtle at first. She saw him, though, and she held her breath. A bullet smacked into the door frame, and Monkey ran to the back of the office. As he ran past the desk, he saw Myrtle there. He looked at her and grinned.

There were six men left out in the street. One peeked out from around a corner, and Slocum shot him dead. The judge hit another one. "Let's get the hell out of here," shouted one of the remaining four. They all ran for their horses. As they did so, Slocum and the judge stepped out into the open.

"Hold it right there," Slocum yelled.

The outlaws stopped in their tracks. They looked at Slocum. They looked at one another. "We can take him," said one.

"Can you take both of us?" said the judge, his voice coming from another direction.

The outlaws, guns in hands, looked toward the judge. He was standing on the sidewalk in front of the sheriff's office with a Colt in each hand. One of the outlaws muttered, "They'll hang us," and they all raised their guns at once. Slocum fired a quick shot, dropping one, and Judge Colter fired two shots. One outlaw fell dead. The other fell back with a crushed shoulder. The fourth one tossed his gun away. "Don't shoot," he screamed. "Don't shoot."

Slocum and Colter looked around the town. They saw no more of the outlaws. They did not know about Monkey in the newspaper office, and they did not know about Beeler. They had no idea how many outlaws had come riding into town. It seemed to be over. "Come on, you two," said Colter.

"I'm hurt," said the wounded badman.

"I'll fetch you a doc when I get the time," said Colter. "Get moving."

He marched the two sorry wretches into the sheriff's office, and put them in a cell and locked the door.

"I'm bleeding to death," said the wounded one.

"Hurry it up then," said Colter as he walked back out into the street. He found Slocum studying the dead bodies.

"I believe these are all former employees of Thornton," Slocum said.

"We might find out from those two in jail what was going on here," said Colter. "I suppose I'd better find a doctor."

A man stepped cautiously out of a doorway, looking around as if to make sure the danger had passed. Colter saw him.

"You there," he said. "Fetch the doc and send him over to the jail." He glanced at Slocum. "Let's go look in on Thornton," he said.

As they walked toward Thornton's office, people began emerging from their hiding places, and the judge ordered several of them to begin gathering up the bodies. The judge and Slocum reached Thornton's office and saw his body in the doorway. They looked at each other. The judge stepped over the body and looked around the office. "His carpetbag is missing," he said. He stepped back into the street just in time to see the doctor with his black bag hurrying toward the jail. "Slow down, Doc," he said, "and I'll walk along with you."

Slocum stood there and looked around. It seemed that it was all over. Snippet and Wilder still had a problem. They had to figure out how to get the land for the railroad, and with Thornton dead, and the deeds tied up in Colter's investigation, they might have quite a wait. But Thornton was dead, and his former outlaw gang was all dead or in jail. Slocum figured that he could ride away from all this in the morning. He would be glad to put Charlotte's Town behind him. He decided to walk over to the newspaper office to see Myrtle.

Monkey had dragged Myrtle to the back door with his gun barrel at her head. When he opened the door and looked outside, he saw no sign of a horse. He couldn't possibly get away that way. He'd have to try the front. There was more than a chance that he'd be seen, but there were horses out there, and he did have the girl as a shield. When the shooting had stopped outside, he knew that the battle was lost. Everyone was dead out there, he figured. He moved to the door, still clutching Myrtle around the throat, still touching her temple with his gun barrel. When he reached the door, he saw Slocum coming toward him.

"Goddamn," he said, jumping back. He thought quickly.

There was only one thing he could do. He shoved Myrtle into the doorway staying behind her, barely peeking out from behind her head. "Slocum," he shouted. "Hold it right there."

Slocum stopped, taking in the situation immediately. "Let her go," he said.

"Not on your life," said Monkey. "I want you to walk over there and get that horse and bring it over here to me. Wait a minute. Shuck your gun belt first."

Slocum unbuckled the belt and let it fall with the Colt to the street. A little puff of dust rose up as it hit the ground.

"All right," said Monkey. "Fetch the horse over here."

Slocum walked slowly over to the nearest horse. It was one of those the outlaws had been riding. He gathered the reins and led the horse to the front of the newspaper office.

"Now let her go," he said.

"I ain't turning her loose till I'm safe out of town," said Monkey. "Maybe not then. Now you back off."

Slocum backed away slowly, keeping his eyes on Monkey. Monkey reached the horse. "Now you get up into the saddle, missy," he said. He held onto her tightly as she climbed aboard. The horse and Myrtle were between Monkey and Slocum. Monkey had a final thought before leaving town. "Slocum," he said, "you've caused us all a whole lot of grief. I think I'll just kill you before I go."

He aimed his gun across the saddle in front of Myrtle. He thumbed back the hammer. There was an explosion, and Monkey's head flew apart. His gun fell to the street, and his legs wobbled. Then he tipped over backward and fell with a thud. Myrtle slipped from the saddle and ran to Slocum, throwing her arms around him. "Oh, my God," she said.

"It's all over now," said Slocum. He looked up toward a second-floor window of the Ballard Hotel and saw Sidney Wilder standing there with his Henry rifle in his hands. Wilder smiled and waved. Slocum waved back. "Come on," he said to Myrtle, "I'll take you back to the office." He bent to retrieve his Colt as they walked. Up ahead he saw

Judge Colter step out of the sheriff's office. He had heard the shot and come to see what was happening. Slocum walked Myrtle over there.

"What was that shot?" the judge asked.

"That was Wilder saving my life," said Slocum. "Maybe Myrtle's too."

Myrtle gave the judge the details. "Now," she said, "I have to get back to my office. I have work to do."

"Now?" said Slocum.

"The story's fresh," she said. "I have to get it written. I'll need to interview both of you."

"Not me," Slocum said. "I'm going to get a drink."

"I'll see you later," she said, and headed for her office. Slocum walked toward the saloon. Judge Colter went back into the sheriff's office. The doc had finished bandaging the wounded man's shoulder, so the judge opened the cell door to let the doc out. Then the judge closed and locked the door.

"Is he going to live?" he asked.

"I think so," said the doc.

"That's a shame," said the judge. "You want to come along with me? I'm going to the saloon for a drink."

"Sure. I'll join you."

"Send me a bill for the work you just did," said Colter. "I'll see to it you get paid."

They found Slocum at a table in the saloon with a bottle of good bourbon and a glass in front of him. "You mind some company?" asked Colter. "Or would you rather drink alone?"

"Sit down, Judge," said Slocum. "You too, Doc." He waved an arm at the barkeep and called for two more glasses. The barkeep brought the glasses, and Slocum poured them full, shoving one toward the judge and one toward the doc. Just then Wilder walked in. "Come over here," said Slocum. "Sit down. I owe you a drink." He waved for another glass, got it, and poured it full for Wilder.

They sat in silence for a moment, each one sipping his drink. Then Slocum said, "Well, my job's over. I guess you'll still have to be hanging around to clear up that land deal."

"I don't think they'll be needing me for that," said Wilder. "I'll be moving on. But you just think you're done."

"What are you talking about?" Slocum said.

"While you were in the middle of the fight, I saw a man ride away from Townsend's office carrying that carpetbag. I couldn't get a shot at him, though."

19

"Damn," said Slocum.

"Well," said Colter, "at least we've solved the local problem."

"But we got so damn close, I don't want to let it go at that. I mean to track down that last son of a bitch and bring him back here."

"Which way out of town did he go?" Colter asked Wilder. Wilder nodded his head and jerked a thumb, and Colter glanced in that direction. "He's headed for the capital," he said. "That means that I'll be on his trail too."

"I mean to get started right now," said Slocum. He tossed down the remains of his drink and stood up.

"I won't be far behind you," said the judge.

"I'll ride along with you," said Wilder, "at least for a ways. But this is your game. I'm all done."

"Let's go then," said Slocum. He led the way out of the saloon and down to the stable with Wilder following along. Slocum and Wilder got their horses, saddled them, and paid Sam Black. They were soon mounted up riding out of town. As they moved along, they studied the hoofprints in the road. There was one set that showed the rider had left Charlotte's Town in a hurry, but they soon slowed down and mixed with all the others. There was nothing distinctive about them. Slocum moved ahead in frustration. Wilder rode alongside him not seeming to give a damn.

They had gotten a few miles out of town and were moving down the trail where the rocky hillside rose up to their left. Slocum was not watching the hillside too closely. He figured that the man he was after had continued to move ahead as quickly as possible. He was watching the tracks in the road to see if anyone had started running a horse again. So far there was no indication. All of a sudden a shot rang out, and Wilder's hat was whiffed off of his head.

"Damn," said Wilder.

Wilder and Slocum both dismounted fast and ran for cover. Each man found a rock large enough to hide behind on the side of the road opposite the hill. They were not far from one another.

"Now I'm mad at him," Wilder said.

"Do you know where he's at?" Slocum asked.

"I ain't been able to make him out yet," Wilder answered. "You have any suggestions?"

"One of us could stand up and make a target for him," said Slocum.

"I said I'm mad at him, but that don't mean I'm stupid. That was a rifle he fired."

"Watch the hillside," said Slocum.

He looked around for another place to hide, not too far away from where he was already snugged down. He spotted a small clump of brush just off to his left. He thought that he could make it over there and have enough cover for safety. He stood up and ran. A shot rang out just as he made a dive for the brush. Wilder snapped off three shots from one of his Remingtons.

"You hit anything?" asked Slocum.

"Nah," said Wilder. "But I got him spotted. You see that largest boulder up there? Just to the right of that scrawny little oak?"

"I see it," said Slocum.

"He's behind that," said Wilder.

"It's a long shot for a six-gun," Slocum said.

Wilder looked toward their horses. His was the nearest, and it was standing where Wilder, if he made it over to the horse, could grab his Henry rifle with the horse between him and the outlaw.

"Shoot up there and bother him," Wilder said.

Slocum fired four shots while Wilder ran for his Henry. Wilder grabbed the rifle and jerked it from the scabbard. Then he turned and ran back for cover. Another rifle shot sounded from the hillside, but it did no damage.

"Okay," said Slocum. "You got your rifle. Now what?"

"I'm going to try to scatter some trash down on his head," said Wilder. He took aim for the rocks just above the big rock behind which his quarry was hidden. He fired as rapidly as he could crank the Henry. Loose rocks tumbled down. The man did not appear.

Judge Colter was riding along behind Slocum and Wilder when he heard the shots. He figured that the two had caught up with the outlaw, and he rode forward a little faster. In a short time he could see the gunfight going on up ahead. There seemed to be two men hidden down beside the road and a third up on the hillside. It didn't take much thought to figure out that Slocum and Wilder had been ambushed. At least, it made sense to play it that way. Colter moved to the side of the road and dismounted. He lapped the reins of his horse around a small bush that was growing there beside the road, and he started climbing. He could hear the gunshots continuing as he moved up the rocky hillside. The ground was treacherous just where he started climbing, covered with small, loose rocks. He moved slowly. Better to get there than to slip and fall and have to start all over again.

Beeler cursed himself for missing his first shot. He still had two men down below to deal with, and they were both dangerous men. He knew that. He was in a pretty good position, though. He occupied the high ground, had good cover, and had a rifle. That Wilder had his rifle as well, but he obviously did not have a good shot at Beeler, for he was trying to drive him out of his hiding place by knocking loose small rocks up the hillside. Well, they were annoying, but they would not make him budge. He could stand a bit of a rock shower. He peered out from behind his boulder and took aim at the bush Slocum had run to. He fired into the bush. A shot from the Henry rifle came immediately afterward, and Beeler just managed to duck behind the boulder in time. They had him pegged for sure. He could not move out from behind his rock, and neither could they move from their hidey-holes. It was a Mexican standoff.

"Slocum," said Wilder. "What the hell are we going to do?"

"Your guess is good as mine," said Slocum.

Then Wilder called out in a loud voice, "Hey, you up the hill. Who the hell are you?"

"None of your business," came the response. "If you don't know me, how come you're shooting at me?"

"You son of a bitch," called Wilder, "you shot off my good hat from ambush. We're just defending ourselves."

"What if I say that was a mistake? What if I apologize? Will you both just mount up and ride on?"

"And take a chance that you won't just shoot us down?" said Wilder. "No way. Why don't you come down here in the road and face me like a man?"

"I ain't no fool. I know who you are."

"Aw, come on down," said Wilder.

"You move out in the road first," said Beeler. "Then I might come down to join you."

Judge Colter was on top walking the ridge. He could hear the voices. At first he couldn't make them out, but after a few more steps, he could understand every word. He recognized the voice of Wilder. He wondered why Slocum was silent. He hoped he had not been hit. The last voice of the man on the hillside had been loud and clear, so Colter stooped into a crouch and moved more slowly. He slipped both Colts out of their holsters.

• • •

Slocum glanced up and saw a movement on the ridge. He watched closely. In another moment, he recognized Judge Colter sneaking along toward the ambusher. "Wilder," he said, his voice a harsh whisper.

"What?"

"Look up on top."

"By damn. It's the judge."

"Let's give him a little help," Slocum said. "Distract the bastard that's shooting at us."

Wilder cut loose with his Henry, and Slocum emptied his Colt. He started refilling it while Wilder continued shooting. His Colt loaded again, Slocum resumed firing. Up on the hillside, Beeler crouched tightly behind his boulder. He knew they couldn't hit him as long as he stayed low behind the boulder, but he wondered what the hell they were up to. The firing stopped as abruptly as it had started. He sneaked a peek around the edge of the boulder to see what he could see.

"Don't make a move," came a voice from above.

Beeler turned to look. He saw the judge looking like the angel of death, standing above him with a gun in each hand, a ferocious scowl on his face, the tails of his black coat flapping in the wind. He wondered what he should do. If he dropped his guns, he would taken back to jail. The money would be confiscated. He might be hanged. If not, he would surely spend years, perhaps the rest of his life, in prison. If he tried to down the judge, he could easily be killed. If he got lucky and dropped the judge, he still had the other two down below to deal with.

"Drop the rifle," said the judge.

Beeler thought that he would rather be dead than in prison. He thought he would rather be shot than hanged. He really had no choice. He had to go for it.

"Now," said Colter.

Beeler swung his rifle barrel toward the judge and pulled the trigger, but Colter's shots came faster. Two slugs from the judge's Colts tore into Beeler's chest. Beeler straightened up with a horrible grimace on his face. He leaned back against the boulder and dropped the rifle. Then he slid slowly sideways, leaving a trail of blood on the rock, and fell over dead. Colter walked on down the hillside and checked the body. He stood up to call down to Slocum and Wilder.

"I got him," he said. "Come on out."

Slocum and Wilder walked out into the road and looked up toward the judge.

"Has he got the carpetbag?" Wilder asked.

"I don't see it," said Colter, "but I don't see a horse either. It must be down on the other side. If one of you will ride back down the road a little ways and fetch my horse up here, I'll go down the other side and see if I can find it."

"I'll go," said Slocum. He walked back for his Appaloosa, mounted up, and rode for the judge's horse. Wilder mounted his horse, but sat still watching the judge disappear over the top of the hill. Slocum came back first, leading the judge's horse. Wilder decided to go up the hillside to see if he recognized the dead man. He made the climb, then grabbed the body by the shirt collar and dragged it on down to the road.

"I don't recall his name," he said, "but I seen him in Thornton's office. He's the one I seen riding out of town with the carpetbag too. I guess he must have double-crossed his boss, killed him, and took his money."

Colter was back just a little later carrying the carpetbag. "I unsaddled the horse and turned it loose," he said. "This is full of money all right."

"It was Thornton's money," said Slocum, "but we don't know where he got it. What'll become of it?"

"We'll make an attempt to find out if any of the people he murdered have got any heirs. If we can find them, they'll get the money that was stolen from their deceased relatives. The rest of it will go into the government coffers, I guess."

"I know of two heirs," said Slocum.

"The McGuire children," said Colter. "Yes. Their share will be banked for them. I'll see to that for sure."

"Well," Slocum said, "I have to go back to Charlotte's Town. I left my stuff in the back room of the newspaper office. Then I'll be on my way."

"Where to?" asked Wilder.

Slocum shrugged. "It don't much matter," he said.

"Slocum," said Colter, "I'm going to trust you with this money. Give it to Myrtle, and tell her to bank it and hold it until my return. I have a mess of paperwork to do regarding this case, and I miss my little wife like blazes."

Slocum took the bag. "All right," he said. "So you're headed back to the capital?"

"That I am, and none too soon."

"I'll ride along with you," said Wilder. "I mean to catch the train there for St. Louis."

"So long to both of you," Slocum said. He threw the carpetbag up over his saddle, hanging it on the horn, and headed toward Charlotte's Town. Colter and Wilder started riding toward the capital.

Back in Charlotte's Town, Slocum looked up Myrtle and handed the bag to her, telling her what Colter had said.

"I don't know what made him trust me with all this money," he added.

"I do," she said.

"Well, I'm going to fetch my roll and ride on out."

"Can I buy you one last drink?"

"Sure," he said.

They started walking toward the saloon, and Myrtle asked, "So the judge said he would be coming back to town?"

"About as soon as he finishes up the paperwork, he said."

"Well," she said, "I've got one hell of a big story to work on in the meantime."

20

Drawing near the capital, the judge made an excuse and turned off on a side road, leaving Wilder to travel the rest of the way alone. It wasn't far, though. Colter watched Wilder go, and then he got back on the road. It wasn't far from Judy's Place, and he knew that it would already be closed. When he reached it, he tied his horse around back, then rapped on the back door. In a moment it was opened. Judy was standing there, several wisps of hair hanging down in her face. She smiled when she saw Colter.

"Hello, Ira," she said. "All alone this time?"

"Just me, my dear," he said.

"Well, come on in."

Colter went into the house, and Judy shut the door and latched it. She led the way into the kitchen, where she prepared a plate of food for the judge and put it before him on the table. She poured a cup of coffee and set it on the table. Then she poured herself one and sat down across the table from him. She watched him with pleasure as he ate his meal. Soon they had both finished their coffee. The judge leaned back in his chair and smiled at Judy. Judy stood up and held out a hand. Colter took her hand in his and held it for a moment. Then he pulled it to his face and kissed it. Standing up, he allowed her to lead him into a bedroom.

She released his hand and helped him out of his coat and then his vest. The judge slipped his galluses off his shoulders and slithered out of his shirt. He sat on the edge of the bed, and Judy knelt before him to pull off his boots. She stood up again and began to disrobe. Colter finished stripping in a minute.

They stood naked, looking at one another, smiling. Then Judy crawled into the bed, spread her legs, and held out her arms. Colter crawled in between her legs, lowering his weight on top of her body. She sighed heavily, and he grunted. Her hands went down between them to his crotch, and they grappled with his already engorged cock. They fondled his heavy balls.

"Oh, oh," said the judge. He tried to thrust himself into her, but without success. She guided the rigid tool into the proper place, and he rammed it home.

"Ahh," she said. "Oh, yes."

He shoved himself deep into her, all the way in, and she responded with an upward thrust of her pelvis. Then the judge began pounding against her, in and out of her, and she responded in rhythmic humps. Their bodies made a slapping noise as they came together.

Back in Charlotte's Town, Myrtle Gilligan sat late in her office writing away on the penultimate segment of the story of Jobe Thornton. She gloried in it. She knew that there would be one more installment, when the judge had finished up his report and the issue of the money was finally settled. But that one would be anticlimactic. This one, the one she was writing right now, was the one she had waited for so long. She would never write another story that would give her the pleasure she was receiving from this one.

The night was late, and Slocum rode slowly and aimlessly. He had no destination. He thought about all the characters he had met in Charlotte's Town. Most of them he would never miss. He would be just as happy had he never met them. A few of them had been all right, and even fewer had been downright interesting. All in all, though, he'd had enough of Charlotte's Town and its inhabitants to last him a lifetime. He did not think he would be riding back this way again.

Judge Colter finally arrived at his home. His lovely young wife ran to meet him with open arms. Their bodies came together, and their arms wrapped around each other. At last she loosened her embrace just enough to tilt her head back, and he kissed her long and lovingly. When the kiss at last ended, the judge said, "My sweet little darling, my delicious loving wife, I've missed you so terribly much."

"Oh," she said, "me too. I'm so glad you're home at last."

Watch for

SLOCUM AT HANGDOG

334th novel in the exciting SLOCUM series
from Jove

Coming in December!